Things With Feathers

stories of hope

Third Flatiron Anthologies
Volume 10, Book 30, Fall/Winter 2021

Edited by Juliana Rew
Cover Art by Keely Rew

Things With Feathers: Stories of Hope
Third Flatiron Anthologies
Volume 10, Fall/Winter 2021

Published by Third Flatiron Publishing
Juliana Rew, Editor and Publisher

Copyright 2021 Third Flatiron Publishing
ISBN #978-1-7362848-2-7

Discover other titles by Third Flatiron:

License Notes

www.thirdflatiron.com

Contents

5

Dream Eater

by Nemma Wollenfang

Sleep, sweet dreamers. Sleep until the world is gone...

As the neighbourhood descends into the cathartic embrace of slumber, I hover over all—a wraith on feather wings that circles and soars. None see me, none would. Not even if they were to peek through the thick curtains of their cosy homes. For I am as black as the night.

A moonless sky veils the world as I flap my great wings and fly. The streets of London are quiet at this hour, tranquil as a church's crypt. Westcott Avenue disappears below, and I glide over terraced rows into Newport Street. Always looking, always listening . . .

So much gold. And all of it mine? This will solve everything!

The children have sprouted wings? Ernest will have a fit. . .

I'll paint the house in rainbows, that's what I'll do. Capital idea!

Nonsensical threads of half-formed dreams drift from open windows, like waving worms ready to be plucked. There are so many, and all are so lush and juicy.

The human mind is an imaginative place, more so in this era of invention, and here they are ripe for the picking.

Selecting a target, I dive and peck, ensnaring a golden ripple in my razor beak.

It squirms, releasing a high-pitched squeal like the tremble of wind chimes. Its eldritch light flickers as it struggles to withdraw into the safety of its window. It's useless, I have a firm grip. With a rough yank, I tear it away and gulp. The taste is divine: *lilac and jasmine, honey and milk,* ambrosia of the Gods. *More. . .* I circle and veer back, spying another waving form.

I feed on thoughts of summer sands and winter slopes, I feed on child's laughter and a lover's kiss, I feed on far-flung hopes and distant horizons. *More. . .*

I feed on all and leave nothing behind. Except for the nightmares, those they can keep.

And yet the hunger persists.

. . .

When dawn crests the dew-coated streets with its fresh glow, the sleepy inhabitants begin to stir. That is my cue, my signal to retreat. One shiver, and in a waterfall rush my body takes on the tangibility of solid form. Wind, rain, icy chill—senses hone to a glaring new spectrum.

I have not reaped enough to settle my gut, but the rising sun means an end to the hunt.

With innards now grumbling twice over for nourishment, I seek shelter in the gnarled branches of an old oak tree, where insects scatter and brown leaves rustle. Lifting an unkempt wing—plumage ragged, thick with lice—I tuck my head into the crevice of a wingpit and try to rest. Sleep does not come easy most days, and now not at all. The hunger is far too strong.

At midday I venture out into the world again, flying over road and field in search of something, anything, to sate that gnawing ache. Physical food now, something solid.

Dream Eater

The cobbles are damp, and the grass is soggy, a spray of rain swirls in the air. Traffic blasts below; steam trains and cars and trams with their shrieking horns. Noxious grey smoke consumes the sky, and I swerve to avoid the rotating propellers of low-flying airships.

I hate the damp. I hate the noise. I hate the thick patches of industrial smog.

I hate the people.

Spoilt. The lot of them. With hungers so easily sated, sleep so easily gained.

Into a park I glide, hovering above a dozen wooden tables ringed by trees. All are occupied—the lunchtime rush—and all are oblivious. My belly roils, in anticipation now. That is the way with physical forms; they require regular maintenance of the gastric and cardiac systems. Not like that evanescent spectre that lurks the dark hours—my other ethereal self. Though that, too, requires more than it ever used to. There was a time, long ago, when one dream could sate that famishment for nigh on a year. No more, it seems. Both hungers cry out now, unified in distress. Both constantly demand more. Neither is easy to assuage.

Chatter from the picnic tables rises up in a cacophony of noise.

"We should invite Margery when we head for Cornwall. She'd simply love it there."

"No, I told him. That price is simply too high!"

"Look, can we just have a nice, quiet luncheon, Cuthbert? *Please.*"

No one sleeps in the daylight hours. No one dreams. So I cannot feed that hunger. The other, however, the gastric rumble. . . must make do with what scraps can be pilfered.

I choose my spot with precision—a family group on the outer edge who have plenty of food to spare and a little one with clumsy hands. I tumble, crashing into the grass nearby.

13

The child spots me first as I hobble their way. It wears a flat cap, breeches, and braces over a white shirt. "Mamma, what is that?" He points with a jammy finger.

His mother turns and starts. "It's sick, honey. Don't touch it. Come away."

With ushering haste, the family depart—leaving their bounty to the birds. I am not the only one to target them, others are already present: crows and jackdaws, rooks and magpies. All the carrion feeders vie for the prizes on offer with snapping beaks and scratching claws.

Mine! Mine! Mine!

More! More! More!

They squawk in angry protest as I approach, flapping their wings as if they mean to beat me away with air currents alone. I will not be beaten back. I will have my share.

Trudging close, I release a hoarse wheeze. It rattles, phlegmy and sickly, like a chimney sweep's cough. The other raptors back off, and with unhappy clacks they take wing and vanish. None stay, none would—for I am the bird who other birds shun.

The bread is coarse, half-stale and sticky with jam. I gobble everything, crumbs and all, pecking in the grass to retrieve strays.

Perhaps it is the scraggly coat that the other creatures fear, perhaps it is the sharper than average caw. Perhaps they simply sense that something is different, inherently wrong.

I am wrong. I feed on slumber's music.

The bread is insufficient, as always. The taste on my tongue is bitter.

I hobble to the next table, and the next. Nothing at either, and as I creep closer their occupants subtly pack up and flee. The third table is already leaving when I arrive. I have better luck there. An abandoned hamper! With. . . nothing but a napkin inside. Humph.

"What is *that*?" a voice cries. "Ugh! It's hideous!"

14

I look up to see a pair of parasol-bearing women staring down with distaste.

Fashion is transitory, changing with every era. And these two wear the tightly boned corsets, frilly bustles, and ribbon-like fascinators favoured by the women of this time.

"What's wrong with it?" the first voice continues. It belongs to the skinny blonde with ample ringlets and a bright pink pelisse—the one who stands far too close to an abandoned crust.

With a flap, I nip at her toes. *Mine!*

She yelps and jumps back. I feast.

Other words fall from their lips as I peck, in half-mutters, words like 'deformed' and 'ugly' and 'diseased.' They see what I am, even if they do not understand. They see the grotesque, black varmint. I've heard it all before, could not care less to hear it again.

A pink handbag swings my way. I shriek, falling back, and flap and flap and flap!

"It's just a crow, Tabbi," the other girl says, the brunette. "Leave it alone."

Another *caw* works its way from my throat, a disgruntled and gritty croak.

"Sounds like it's dying," the blonde girl mutters. She seems relieved.

"Poor thing." Her companion shifts closer and crouches nearby. A lonely hand rises.

"Don't touch it!" the blonde frets, her disgust plain. "You don't know where it's *been*."

The brunette does not listen. She does not cringe or strike out. She is the only one who has ever dared approach.

Mute with surprise, I let her reach. . . and touch. . . and stroke. *No human has ever. . .*

"Soft," she says, "like silk. . . "

Her touch is satin, a warm sensation that seeps through feather into flesh and bone.

I remember this one, I fed from her. Her dreams were succulent and satisfying.

The memory of fresh-baked cookies, eaten with chocolate milk as a child. . . A mother's kiss, rich in unconditional affection. . .

"Rhoda," her friend whines.

Ah, a name. With it I am ensnared. Magnetic beauty spills from her unwavering gaze. The colours of Rhoda's irises are sublime. Gentle brown and jaded green and moss—earthy hues. Hypnotised, I stare. My eyes are reflected in hers too—twin mirrors of black ice.

And I think I see her shiver.

"Come away, Rhoda," the other female insists. She looks as uneasy as other humans do around me. *She senses the underlying wrongness. . . does the brunette not?*

With a blink and a shake, Rhoda breaks her trance and stands. For a moment I feel strangely bereft, but before she departs she reaches out. There is something in her hand.

"Here," she says. "You look like you need it."

A handful of bread crusts are tossed to the ground. Then she leaves.

Food. . . she gave food. No human has ever done this before. No human has ever shown such simple kindness. And the bread tastes somehow better for it.

. . .

That night I find her again—Rhoda, the brunette with the bread. It is not hard. I hear the high chime of her dream chords as they wave and sing, glowing in the dark. And I remember their call. Her window is open, its lace curtains billow into the cool night like gossamer veils.

Something is amiss.

Clouded in thunder, she writhes and moans—a helpless victim of her darker mind. Vicious spiked leeches wind their way into the air alongside the golden dream threads, like weeds amongst a garden of roses. But unlike the gold they do not wave and sing. No, they constrict their counterparts, squeezing like ivy and piercing until the innocent gold squeals.

Boas ensnaring fragile prey. . .
Rocks beating china. . .
Executioners tightening the noose. . .

With an irritable flap, I snap at the air, diving and pecking. I snatch one. It growls. An unfamiliar rumble I return in kind. With hard yanks, I fight to haul it back as my wings beat air. Pulling, pulling. The grey worm flails, growing taut. Sharp, steel grey barbs abrade my feathers. The pain is tolerable, the damage minimal. All I need do is groom again later.

It gives with the high screech of nails on chalkboard.

Reeeeeeeeeeeee. . .

I gulp it down. The taste is repugnant—a cystic tang reminiscent of puss-filled boils and weeping sores. But the golden thread is now free, free to sway and sing its haunting crystal song. The girl seems to calm. Night gentles. But more begin to rise. *More. . .*

I wait for the nightmares. . . and strike!

Visceral tastes butcher my tongue: bubbling tar and foul egg sulphur, organic decay and smoky ash. Destructive tastes, vulgar tastes.

Maggots feast on a rotting carcass. . .
Dripping canines and glowing red eyes. . .
Volcanic magma. . .
A panicked breath. . .

No ambrosia but the rotten perfume of putrefaction. Somehow, they still satisfy and that other hunger abates.

No longer smothered, her seedling dreams sprout and grow, blooming into fully fledged glowing reeds.

Tinkling laughter. . .
Poetic rhyme. . .
The sensation of sunlight on skin. . .

No longer gold but silver. And such a silver I have never before seen, for it is so much more than that. Sparkly, shining, crackling with life. The mercury threads wave with the sinuous grace of flowing water. Their lengths fragment with microscopic prisms of diamond dust. Her dreams are exquisite, *she* is exquisite.

. . .

The next day I follow her. I cannot say why.

Hopping from branch to branch in the gnarled oak trees above, I track Rhoda as she goes about her day. She never looks up. Why would she? Her world is on the ground.

I watch as she walks the land in a ruffled mauve dress and high clacking heels. I watch through a high window as she drinks tea and talks to other ladies in a great wood-panelled hall, where white-clad males in mesh masks do battle with giant needles. I watch as she departs to eat a meagre lunch on an outdoor bench. I watch as she smiles.

She intrigues me, in a way no human ever has— *this woman with a kind soul.*

And while she does not look directly at me as she passes my perch, her hand slips into her purse and out come the crumbly crusts. With a subtle flick, she tosses them.

I gobble all. Why would I not? They are given freely, and the taste is not so bad.

This process continues for many days. I find I crave the sweet dream threads less and less. The acrid nightmares do well enough to hold that hunger at bay, and the time I spend with her seems to sate what remains of that visceral side of me. It is as if she emanates sunlight, and I bask in its nutritious glow. The hearty bread helps too; it quiets the other nagging ache in a way it never fully used to. And because of that, once again I manage to sleep at dawn.

I wonder why. What has changed?

Dream Eater

My life has fallen seamlessly into a new routine. By night I stay by her side, leeching away the cloying darkness. Peace is all she knows in sleep, and happiness, and light. Without the darkness that is all there is. Sometimes, I wish I could join her there—in the Edens she creates. Instead I stand sentinel, her stalwart guard, her Uriel with the flaming sword. Her eyes flit behind closed lids and fingers twitch as she softly moans. I marvel at the boneless grace of her slumber—such peace is rare in the waking world.

By day I venture out into the world, flying over street and park, gliding around Big Ben, flitting between dirigibles and dancing in the wind-currents from their propellers. The cobbles are no longer just damp but a glistening palette of silver. *Like her new dreams.* The blast of traffic is no longer shrill but as melodic as music. Horses whinny, people talk, machinery rolls and grinds. Rain still swirls, but I shower in its refreshing chill. And the air is crisp and clear.

I love the rain. I love the music. I love the flight.

I love the people.

They are not so bad. I leave their dreams alone.

The park and its bounties I abandon to the other needier creatures, and I take to roosting in my Rhoda's rose garden, where I have a clear vantage of her bedroom window. She notices, of course. The female has a sharp eye. But she does not groan at this new development as others might, nor does she swat or shoo. She smiles, she always smiles.

"You're looking much better," my girl says one morn as she winds in ringlets. "Your feathers are glossy, your throat is clear, and your eyes sparkle like beady black beetles."

It is true. In these past days I have never been healthier. The thick infestation of lice has sloughed away like a shed husk, leaving my skin a healthy pink. My wings gleam with the rainbows of oil; they now repel the rain. And when I caw, the sound is almost symphonic.

I am as I used to be, in days long past, a fine and admirable specimen of ancient lore. Back then, my luminous wings had been muses to bards and painters and sculptors alike.

"I wonder," she says, "do you have a name, little one?"

Of course I cannot reply, and she does not expect me to. Even if I could, I would have no ready answer. The ones I once bore have long since faded from memory.

At night, as she sleeps, I sit on her sill and sift through her consciousness the way a panner sifts through river grit for sparks of gold. Only, when I find gold, I leave it be. I let the threads sprout and bloom and wave and sing, eventually planting a few seeds of my own.

The fledgling sprouts mature, and as they do a new spectre appears beside her dreaming avatar.

A man.

An echo of myself.

This new form is uncomfortable for me. The hair is raven-black but too thin and fine to be feathers. The body is lean and muscular but too tall. The clothes are tight and constricting. I straighten the shirt and pull at the ivory silk cummerbund with unfamiliar fingers.

I wonder if she will like me this way. The thought that she will not is distressing.

From where she stands amongst the swaying dream grass, donned in her mauve corset and bustle skirt, she turns, and sees. . . and she smiles and says, "Hello."

Relief. I stop my uneasy shifting.

Approaching with a ballerina's elegance she raises a hand. . . and touches. . . and strokes.

"Soft," she says, "like silk. . . "

My cheek leans into her satiny palm. Even though it is unreal, even though it cannot physically be so, her touch soothes and heats my new flesh. Igniting a part of me I thought long dead. And, emboldened, I return the smile that she first gave. "Hello."

. . .

Like a botanist I tend to Rhoda's dream garden, weeding and nurturing through the night—with hands this time, not beak and talons. I care for her dreams. I eat her nightmares.

She deserves no less than the utmost devotion.

Deep in slumber, her garden is a rich amassment of flora that simply cannot be. Trees that walk, and vines that curl and plait. Psychedelic blooms flower amidst lush grass that sings. Pollen fragrances the air with a lilac mist as we walk hand in hand, while shafts of sunlight sparkle over everything and dragonflies chime and dance the *Chaconne*.

I lead her to a rope swing, where she propels her legs back and forth as she teases and laughs with me.

She calls me Leith, *her* Leith. The gift of a name is something I never thought to receive.

Within her mind, I take the ropes to still her swing, then, looking deep into those moss-laden eyes, I kiss those plump lips in a way I never could in waking day.

The white gold threads sing for us, their music like the melodic tremble of harp strings. Their tunes are soothing and honeyed, and I pull her up so we can press our bodies close and sway to their ethereal songs.

The feel of her is addictive, her essence is enthralling. I take her in my arms and never let go. In this way we build our own world—Adam and Eve of nowhere.

Her friend will always taste the bitter bile of nightmares, but she, the girl with a golden heart, her dreams will be saccharine forever.

Sleep, sweet dreamer. Sleep until the world is gone. . .

###

About the Author

Nemma Wollenfang's work has appeared in several venues, including *Beyond the Stars, Abyss & Apex, Cossmass Infinities,* and Flame Tree's Gothic Fantasy series. She is a recipient of the Speculative Literature Foundation's Working Class Writers Grant and can be found on Facebook, Twitter, and at her website: www.nemmawollenfang.co.uk

*****~~~~~*****

The Soul of Trees

by Emily Dauvin

Hua wondered how she was going to look after Grandfather's garden. She walked back from the train station, her Mom safely boarded on her way back to the city. Hua felt a bit giddy to be staying here at Grandfather's house in the country. This only made her feel guilty. She was supposed to be mourning. The pothole-pocked gravel road was empty, and only a few houses in the rural area lined the road. She had walked this way many times with Grandfather as a child, returning from the city to eat mochi in his beautiful garden.

A grey tabby cat sat on the fence next to the road. Hua was writing her resignation email to work in her head, but she still had the prototype of the cat translator she had been working on in her pocket. She clipped it to her ear and beckoned to the cat. It turned up its nose and paced along the wall. The translator picked up a meow, translating it to "I will not be pet by strangers."

"Fine," Hua said back to the cat. "But I know you come to the garden every day, we won't be strangers for long."

Hua turned up the lane to where her Grandparents had lived, and where she would be staying until the dreaded realtor came. She had convinced her Mom to let her look after the house and the expansive garden that Grandfather had spent his whole life cultivating until Mom decided to sell.

It didn't feel right to sell the house, with Grandfather resting in the garden, but Mom always thought practically. She couldn't see how either she or her mom could keep the house while still working at their jobs in the city. Hua had to find a way to stay close to this house. She had spent so many happy summers here. She didn't have long before Mom would want to sell, and without her job, she wouldn't be able to afford to live here long. Mom, angry that Hua wanted to quit her job, had decided Hua would be responsible for the bills until the house sold.

The windows were all dark in the house. It was lonelier now than she remembered, now that all of her family had gone home. She walked through the rooms, lighting them up. The kitchen was clean after the last tea that she and Mom had shared in the garden. Mom would never leave a dirty dish in the sink. The glass dish that Grandfather always had filled with candy was empty, cleaned out by one of her Uncles after the memorial. The tea set that they always used when Hua came to visit was away in the cabinet.

Hua sat down at the table and surveyed the room where they had shared many meals at holidays. She had never been alone in this house. Hua had many memories of Mom, and Grandfather and her Aunties and Uncles in this room. They had all come, those who were still with them, to share in the memory of Grandfather. They did a ceremony yesterday. They sprinkled his ashes around the ginkgo tree in the garden and fixed a plaque to the trunk.

Hua had tried to be strong and support Mom during the ceremony, but the sight of the bright red goji berries in the garden brought tears to her eyes. Grandfather always waited until Hua could come to visit to pick them, losing most of them to the birds in the meantime. The talk of the family afterwards, as they stood picking the berries, made Hua cry worse.

"The house would fetch a good price, but he left it to Chun and Hua."

Hua wanted to come up to them and tell them off for eating the berries, but a fierce wind came through the garden and whipped through the ginkgo's leaves, making the boughs shake. Hua took a breath. Grandfather didn't want her to fight with her family. She would be alone with the house soon enough.

Hua sat down at her computer in the dining room. She had to write her resignation email. She had been so excited when she had gotten the job at Liu. They made high-tech products, and it had been an amazing job out of university, especially when she was assigned to the cat translator project. She had only worked at Liu for a couple of years, but she had come home in tears almost every night. Her boss was awful, and her coworkers were worse. Hua knew she could do the work, the programming was easy, and she had been top of her class, but then, Grandfather got sick, and everything in life felt so hard.

Hua typed up the email and clicked send before she could second-guess herself. She had already argued her case to Mom, she didn't need to argue with herself. She would live here as long as she could. Feel close to Grandfather as long as she was able, while she worked out how to support herself without her job.

. . .

The flowers were wilting. The summer heat started to soak the garden in its warm rays even before Hua could wake up. Her lack of routine was making her wake later and later. Every morning when Hua stumbled to the kitchen to make her coffee, she looked out over the garden that was already fainting in the heat.

She would step out with the watering can, but it seemed like some plants were still not getting enough water, and others were possibly getting too much. There were dead blossoms on some plants that might have to come off. Hua tried to look all of these things up, but there were too many plants. She couldn't identify them all, and she just didn't know enough.

"No wonder Mom said I couldn't do it," she said to the potted lemon on the patio. "It's such a beautiful garden, but it won't be by the time I'm through with it."

A soft ray of sun shone on the golden plaque on the ginkgo tree. Hua knelt down in front of the tree, looking at Grandfather's name on the plaque.

"Help me, Grandfather. You tried to teach me about the plants when you were here, but I didn't learn enough. I don't want to ruin your legacy, please guide me."

Hua remained kneeling. She tried to listen to the wind blowing through the tree and to the birds chirping and hopping around in the hedges. Grandfather couldn't answer. She would give so much just to hear his voice again.

A soft meow came from behind her. The grey tabby cat that lived down the road came slinking through the grass up to her.

"Hello, little kitty," Hua said, running her hands along his sleek back. "Will you talk to me today?" The cat meowed again. She had sent back the prototype of the translator. "Hm... I wonder if I could find a way to understand the flowers."

. . .

Hua knelt next to the hostas planted in the shady spot next to the house. She'd been working on the prototype of a flower translator. As her first test, she pressed the earpiece of her prototype to turn it on.

"Okay, I'm giving you some water now. Can you tell me when to stop?" Hua poured water down around the hostas waiting to hear something in the earpiece. She knew the hostas best, she had taken a particular interest in them as a child. Perhaps that was due to the little fairy garden that her Grandmother had built among them out of little sticks.

"Cough. Enough! And would it kill you to bring some of that compost over here?"

Hua couldn't believe it. Did it actually work? "What did you say?"

"You heard me." The voice came from the white and green striped leaves in front of her.

"Oh wow! I could kiss you, hosta! This could be my ticket to staying here!"

"Don't. There was a slug here this morning."

. . .

Hua glanced at her phone vibrating on the desk next to her. It was Mom again. She had spent the last week working so hard she kept missing calls. She sighed as she turned away from her work and picked up the phone.

"Hi, Mom."

"Hi, Hua. Have you been eating well?"

Hua's eyes were drawn to the stack of empty noodle cups piled behind her lap top. "Yes, Mom, I've been cooking."

"And what have you been working on? Have you found a new job?"

Hua looked at the code on her screen. She hadn't wanted to share with Mom yet, but Mom would get it out of her, anyways. "I've been working on something for myself. A flower translator."

"What is that?"

"Like the cat translator, but for flowers. They send out vibrations too, I just need to translate them."

"Hua, you really should come back. I'll get my brother to come and look after the place. He can handle selling the house."

"But Mom, I really think the translator will work."

"Really? Show me then, what have you got?"

Hua got up and picked up the ear piece. "Okay, but it's still early days here. This lemon on the patio gets really dry. Let's see what it says."

Hua knelt down next to the lemon. It said nothing. "Here, let me try giving it some water, it should tell me when to stop."

Mom was silent over the phone.

Hua poured water over the dry soil. She poured more than she knew she should, waiting for the lemon to say something.

"I don't hear anything, Hua. Is it working?"

"No. It's not. I can get the hostas to talk. They were telling me all about this frog that used to live there. I'm working on it though, Mom. I swear. It could be a big hit. You know how popular plants are now. People will want this."

"If you say so, Hua." Mom's voice sounded disappointed. "Just don't wait too long to find a job if you need one. Oh. And I got in touch with a realtor, one that knows the area. They should be over in a couple of days to take pictures, so you should tidy up a bit before, alright?"

Hua hung up the phone. Inside, the house was still lit up. She could see the mess that she had made of dirty dishes and clothes strewn on the floor. Most of them didn't fit her anymore. She had lost weight and hadn't kept up with the cleaning. There were piles of unpaid bills on the kitchen counter. She probably could only afford another month here. She was running out of money for food, and she had been paying the bills on the house. The translator needed to work; otherwise more than just her pride was on the line, she would have to go back to the city and stay with Mom until she got another job. And the house would be gone. Even with the garden not looking like it did when Grandfather was alive, it was still beautiful, and the house too. It wouldn't last long on the market.

Hua bent over the lemon on the patio again, to make sure the extra water was draining. She picked up a cough on the ear piece.

"Is that you, lemon?"

It returned a weak cough again into the earpiece. Hua pressed it, trying to figure out if it was still working. The earpiece pinged. The translator was getting there. It had to be. Coughs were communication, she just needed to fine tune it.

She walked back to the hostas under the shade of the house. She could hear them humming to themselves. It worked with the hostas, but that was her test plant. She knew them well. She needed to program the earpiece for each kind of plant. And it might be that some were more willing to talk than others.

. . .

Hua had been working on the flower translator for weeks. She stepped out into the garden and listened to the chorus of voices coming from each blossom and shrub that she passed. The flowers bobbed in the soft wind, soaking in the soft dappled sunlight coming through the leaves of the ginkgo tree.

Mom would be coming today to visit, and probably to urge Hua to come back to the city again. The realtor had taken the pictures, and there had already been a few showings, but Hua had hope. Maybe she wouldn't sell if she could see how close Hua was getting. Hua would show Mom the progress she had made with the translator. She had brought it over to a few neighbours' gardens to test with their plants as well. They all thought she was crazy, but they were starting to hear rumblings about the cat translator that was coming out soon, so they let her go ahead, even with some skepticism on their part.

She had sent out a few emails to some companies too, trying to get someone to pick up the technology. After many sleepless nights compiling the data, a few had actually gotten back to her, hoping to do their own research on the flower translator as well.

Hua surveyed the calling flowers, trying to decide what she should attend to first. The hosta nearest her was crying out, she knelt beside it and stroked its wide green leaves.

"The snails!" it cried.

"Oh!" Hua said, looking beneath the leaves for a few pesky snails.

A pot of mint next to her gave a polite cough, "More water, please. The sunlight off that gold thing gives me too much light in the morning!"

Hua saw what the mint was referring too. It was the plaque on the ginkgo tree. Hua picked up the mint and moved it over.

At the sight of the watering can, many other flowers called for water. Hua heard her name. She looked around. No one was around.

"Did you call for me?" she asked the potted lemon, which had finally begun to talk to her.

"Only for water, some time ago. I could do with some compost too."

Hua poured the water onto the soil until the lemon told her to stop.

"Would anyone here know my name?"

"If we knew your name we might get some better care around here!"

The rising voice of the lemon gave the earpiece of the translator some feedback. Hua adjusted it in her ear.

"Many of us have seen you before, walking in the garden with your grandfather. He didn't need that earpiece to talk to us."

The lemon seemed to wave her leaves in the breeze. Hua gave a slight bow and returned to the task of distributing can after can of water from the well.

She heard her name again. It came from right before her. The ginkgo shivered its fan-shaped leaves and

30

beckoned her forward. It was unmistakable, the ginkgo was calling her.

"Do you know who I am?" Hua asked.

"Yes, little Hua. You spent many summers with me. We shared bites of mochi and picked the goji berries off the branches before the birds could get them all."

"Grandfather!"

Hua knelt next to the tree, the grass prickling her knees.

"I did not think I would be able to speak to you again for quite some time," Hua said, looking up into the boughs of the tree, blue sky and sunlight visible between the fluttering leaves. She felt the tears well up in her eyes. Hua couldn't wait for Mom to arrive, she would be so happy to hear her father's voice again.

She placed her hands on the trunk of the tree, feeling the soul inside through the rough bark beneath her hands. The translator gave a soft ping to indicate it was working.

About the Author

Emily Dauvin lives on an acreage near Bladworth, Saskatchewan, with her husband, cats, and horses. This is her first publication. In the summer she enjoys gardening and hiking. In the winter she finds more time for knitting, weaving, and baking. You can find her on Facebook or on Instagram @emily_dauvin

*****~~~~~*****

Adventures in the Spiritual Lost-and-Found

by Paula Hammond

The cherry strudel's too hot to eat, but I bite into it anyway—distracted as always. I juggle the scorching pieces of fruit between my tongue and the roof of my mouth until it's finally cool enough to swallow, almost choking myself in the process.

Marei stops mid-sentence and looks at me, horrified. "Jesus, Honey, you okay?"

I chug a mouthful of cola and let the ice sloosh around my mouth. I know how I must look. Drawn. Tight-lipped. Unfocussed.

"Burn yourself, huh?" she says in that tone she uses when she's trying not to show how worried she is. "Boy, that's gotta hurt. Get you more ice?" She gives me a piercing look, then stomps off to the counter.

I think she suspects. Sometimes I see her eyeing me up, trying not to ask.

. . .

It's been getting harder and harder: staying in the here and now. Today, nothing seems to work, and I know, with absolute certainty, that I'm going to see Them. Really see Them. Not as shadowy forms flitting on the edge of my consciousness but in the full, terrible weight of their regard. And when that happens, I will lose my mind.

Marei plonks the cup of ice down on the chipped formica with a grunt. "Now, Honey, try not to break a tooth on that, huh?" she says teasingly.

I blink and look at her. The writhing shapes make it hard to focus. I try to see past Them, to Marei. The pungent scent of her coconut hair oil, her shiny cheeks—never any makeup—those black, thrift-store overalls and insanely painted nails. Rainbow sparkles today. This is a woman who is so wonderfully, perfectly real that just being with her makes me smile. I meet her no-nonsense stare, and, as we connect, the door closes. The shapes dissipate and, for the first time all day, They leave me alone.

I've known Marei since we were geek-kids bonding over comics and cult TV. She was plain old Mary back then, but, apparently, Marei has more 'Oh, My!'

I've always tried hard to fit in, but she's never cared. She works off-and-on, earning just enough to pay the rent, blowing the rest on books and bizzaro junk she calls antiques. "Seriously, Honey," she always says, "I could get hit by a bus tomorrow. I'm not gong waste one second on some bull someone else thinks is important."

But it was me who was hit by the bus. I was dead for a full minute. In a coma for a year.

It wasn't like the films. I didn't have any out-of-body experiences. I didn't hear family and friends whispering by my bedside while I was comatose. One second I was jogging through fume-laden traffic, the next I was coming round gagging, with a tube rammed down my throat.

When you've spent 12 months on your back, you don't just get up. You have to rebuild your body one twitching, aching second at a time. I was so eager to get my life back that I didn't dare talk about Them. The things that called to me from the cold sterility of the therapy room. The things only I could see.

At night, I would lie in that mind-fuzz between sleep and wakefulness and feel their rough, pustulant fingers, prickling their way along my body. Their icy breath filling my nose with the smell of sulphur and dust. I'd fight my way back to consciousness with a knot of fear in my gut that doubled me over.

I still start every day like that. And I still know how crazy it's going to sound to anyone else.

I stare at Marei and she arches an eyebrow, Spock style. It's an invitation, so I dive in.

"You remember those things in *Spellsinger*?" I begin. "The things you can only see out of the corner of your eye?"

Marei flashes me a smile. She loves nothing more than book-talk. "Yeah, gneeches."

It's as hard as I thought it would be. I suck in a noiseless breath, pulling faces as I explore the tender blisters on the roof of my mouth. Marei leans forwards and says, expectantly, "Gneeches, huh?"

I smile half-heartedly. For a minute we sit in silence, then Marei squints experimentally, looking pissed that she can't see anything. "Jeez, Kennedy, thought you were never gonna tell me. Got to say, tho'—that hair, those pant-suits, you're definitely channelling Scully more than Mulder."

We talk like in the old days, when we'd exchange books by the bagful and dissect them over smokes stolen from my sister's purse. As we chat, I catch my reflection in the table's cracked varnish and get a rush of nostalgia for the old me.

After—after the accident—I changed jobs, changed apartments, threw myself into work. It helped keep Them at bay. At least for a while.

Now, here I am—a hollow, fearful shell. Carefully corporate, carefully understated. I tell friends that my brush with death has given me a new perspective, but that person you see? She's just window-dressing. A fancy-looking mannequin pretending to be a living, breathing woman.

. . .

Marei starts in that combative way of hers, testing everything I say, trying to find the holes. Soon we're into the meat of it. The whats, the whys, and the hows. We've plenty of source material, but it's all just fiction or wild conspiracy theories.

Marei says we should take the fight to them, but the truth is, there's no 'we.' When it happens, I'll be alone with whatever monsters inhabit the dark spaces.

"Are you kidding me, Kennedy? You know you're never alone." She says this with such certainty I almost believe it. Then I see Them. They're back: crowding the peripheries of my vision. Glowing, obsidian shapes, so close, my skin crawls. I watch Them without looking. I can never look.

Instinctively I flinch. Marei stops mid-flow and scowls. "Honey, you can't go on like this. Let it happen. Face them down."

"Are you insane?" I reply, louder than I intend. "This isn't a game. Critical hit, goodbye Dimensional Shambler."

Marei wrinkles her nose. I know that look. She's on to something. "Gimme your phone."

I unlock it and hand it over.

She dials, and, as she waits for someone to pick up, I sense Them again, scratching at my retinas, trying to get my attention.

Somehow I lose time. Marei is standing over me, offering me the phone. I didn't even hear her make the call. The thought gives me goosebumps.

"C'mon. My place. It's all arranged."

. . .

I'm too zoned-out to argue. Instead I fall into step with Marei's long-legged stride. By the time we're at her apartment I'm panting, new shoes rubbing the skin off the back of my heels, offering an unexpected focus.

She waves me into her studio-come-living room, and I find a seat amongst the paint, twisted wire, canvases, and books.

"So", she starts, looking sheepish, "I called the Aunties."

"You. Can. Not. Be. Serious."

Marei's aunties are the stuff of legend. Not blood relations, you understand. Just women who hang around her mom's, dispensing advice and generally sucking up the hospitality. And they're all as crazy as a bag of cats.

As kids, we gave them nicknames. Rich: a chain-smoker in skyscraper-heels and flowing silk. Angry: round-shouldered, mumbling, fists always clenched. Born-Again: soft, and wide, and smelling of moth balls. Wild: a teller of tall-tales, doer of impossible things, with a hip-flask of brandy stashed in her purse. Sporty: habitually bouncing on the balls of her feet as though someone's about to shout 'go.' Earth-Mother: a human wind-chime of costume jewelry, swathed in riotous fabrics.

"Which one?" I ask warily.

She clears her throat. "All of them."

By the time they arrive I'm hyperventilating. Losing myself. The real world has become mist, and I can feel Their fingers on my shoulders, like sandpaper ants running up and down my arms. And, there, clearer than it's ever been, is the gateway to their realm—a boiling cauldron of crimson, dragging me ever closer.

The Aunties are like a gestalt organism. They all talk at once. No ones listens. Through the jangle of over-sized bangles and the fug of Channel Number 5 I hear Born-Again arguing with Marei. Sporty cuts in, "Cut the crap, Patience, you know we can't do this unless we're six. It's now or never. We're losing her."

Marei leans close. "Just relax, Honey. The Aunties have got it figured—got a plan. Just focus on the gateway. They'll do the rest."

I follow Marei's advice. I close my eyes, take a deep breath, and let myself drift.

The cold is a shock. I hadn't expected it to be cold. I snap my eyes open and find myself in the eye of a storm. Around me spins a tornado of light, the cloud formed by faces twisted into unnatural shapes, mouths open in silent screams. Something touches me, and I spin round to find Marei beside me.

"Looks like we're not in Kansas anymore," she says, grinning. Then, she catches sight of the wall of dead-eyes and gaping mouths, and the humor drains from her face.

"How? How are you here?"

"It's. . . complicated. . . but you know how we always joked that the Aunties were like some sort of tea-fueled coven?. . . " she lets the sentence trail off.

"You didn't say anything!"

Marei snorted. "Wild said she'd turn me into a frog. Besides, you wouldn't have believed me." I wanted to argue, but it was true. The post-accident me wouldn't have.

"So what now? How do we fight Them?"

"We don't. This is a rescue mission."

"What?"

"*You*, Kennedy. We've come to rescue *you*. The bit of you that got left behind in this spiritual lost-and-found when they brought you back from the dead."

It's a throwaway comment, but, instantly, I know it's true. Whatever piece of me is here, it's been pulling at me all this time, trying to make itself complete.

She takes my free hand, and suddenly I can see them. The Aunties. Lined up in front of us like a Wild West posse. Not quite corporeal, but solid enough for me to notice Sporty glance back and give a weird hand signal.

She used to be a marine, so I guess this is shorthand for 'saddle-up troops.'

The Aunties step forward into the swirling wall of flesh. As they press into it, it's the sound that hits me first. An abattoir of terrified pigs, squealing as they bleed out. Then comes the smell. Excrement, spilled guts, bleach. I retch, and my mouth fills with half-digested pie.

Marei pulls me forward. I don't want to go. I've spent so long fighting *not* to be here that every atom of my being protests. I try to pull away, but she grips me like a vice. "I hold you, the Aunties hold us. Break the chain, and none of us are getting back," she hisses.

. . .

When I was a kid I would sit in church and listen to the priest rail about hellfire and damnation. About how, if I was bad, Satan himself would come to claim me. I had this idea that he wouldn't just come for me, he'd climb in through my mouth and eat me up from the inside out. I believed so hard that, at night, I'd lie with one hand on my Bible, the other over my face, breathing in my own exhales, practically suffocating trying to keep him out.

I push myself into the wall of lost souls and, once again, I'm that terrified kid. We press on, regardless, and I hear their voices alternately pleading and threatening, denying and confessing. In that moment, I hear things no-one should ever have to hear. Things that will stay with me in my nightmares.

As I squint though that whimpering, undulating layer, I see the Aunties. Big, small, fat, thin. A shimmering line of elderly black ladies, "marching as to war."

I hadn't realized I'd said the lines of the hymn out loud until Marei replied.

"*Onward Christian Soldiers*. You got that too?" I nod, lips clenched, and she answers my unspoken question. "We're connected to them, I guess. Let's just be lucky we're hearing Born-Again's thoughts and not Angry's."

We emerge from the flesh-wall into Nothing. Bright, silent, and glacial. I fall to my knees and jerk Marei down with me. I'm crouched on a 'floor' I can't see, staring, down, into an endless pit of pulsing light. The vertigo of it freezes me.

Marei nudges me and whispers, in a voice tight with tension, "Leap of faith."

Harrison Ford: that moment where Indy has to walk across what looks like an invisible pathway to find the Holy Grail. I've always said that I'd never be able to walk across. Even if I knew the path was there, I'd have to ass-shuffle the whole way. But now, with the Aunties in front of me and my best-friend holding my hand, I've got to get a grip.

As I climb to my feet, the hairs on the back of my neck prickle, and I feel Them. Marei starts to turn, but I yank her back. We mustn't look. Whatever happens. We mustn't look.

The Aunties are ahead of us, and I can tell that they can feel Them too. There's a moment of psychic static, and then they call out "Run!"

We do. We pass the Aunties at a sprint, and I see them wheel to face whatever's behind us.

I still can't see what they see, but I sense their shock. For a moment these indomitable ladies reel. Then I feel them chiding and bolstering each other. The strain of *Onward Christian Soldiers* echoes through my mind as they step towards the chittering hoards on our heels.

In front of us is a figure that looks like something made out of papier-mâché and pipe cleaners. It's a lumpen creature, thin, with skin like crinkled newsprint. There, clasped in its fibrous fingers, is a young girl, so emaciated that her head is bald and her skin clings to her bones like tanned leather. The thing's funnel-like mouth is embedded in her neck and—oh, Lord—it's feeding!

With every vampiric gulp, the girl sobs and tries to pull away—and that's enough. I see red. I charge, howling, hitting it with the full force of my body. We go down together.

I'm back on my feet in an instant and, as it tries to rise, I drive my stiletto deep into its chest. It bucks like a mule. I hear its bones break, but I stamp down, again and again until, finally, it stops thrashing. I keep on stamping until its bodily fluids seep into my canary-yellow court shoes. A $500 price tag, and I don't even care.

I step over its twitching form, bend down, and scoop her up: that little, lost part of me. I want to clasp her to my breast and keep her safe, but she's so light and frail I'm afraid I'll break her. Marei gives my free hand a reassuring squeeze, and we glance back at the Aunties just as all hell breaks loose.

There's a sound, like ice breaking, and the world turns scarlet. A bilious groan echoes through the void and, beyond, I hear the breathy calls of a million bloodless beasts baying in anticipation. A gigantic claw, pitted and scorched, explodes from the ground. Above us rows of tongues, forked and blistered, erupt from the vermillion sky. They flick back and forth, reminding me of snakes trying to catch the scent of prey.

As one, the Aunties raise their hands. In my head, I hear the lines, "Hell's foundations quiver," and for a moment this ethereal Nothing does indeed quiver.

The ladies are on the attack now, arms linked. I see Earth-Mother falter, but the sister at her side holds her steady. Sporty glances back at us and nods. Somehow we know what to do: we sing. Loud and defiant. Our voices become a tide, pushing back the horror. We sing of joy and love. We sing hymns, and ballads, and Aretha Franklin classics. We sing until we're hoarse.

I still can't see what lies beyond the line of fearless Aunties, but I hear the creatures baying and snarling. The floor buckles and gelatinous shapes ooze and form around

41

us. They tug at our feet, crackling like live wires in the gloom.

I should be terrified, but a wave of hope washes over me. With it comes an incredible lightness. A sense of purpose. A sense of me. It's something I haven't felt for a long time.

The battle seems to take forever, but the tide of hope is unstoppable. Slowly, slowly, the nightmare landscape purples, dissolves, and Marei's apartment comes back into focus.

It takes me a while to realize that I'm not holding the little girl anymore, but that's okay. She's back where she's supposed to be—inside me. Whole and healthy, full of childish wonder and innocent joy.

There's a mirror lying amongst the clutter, and once again I catch my reflection. I'm a mess, but, you know, I kinda like it.

Around me, the Aunties are already doing their aunty thing. Fussing about the chaos of Marei's little flat; silently disapproving. Earth-Mother jangles off to make tea. I clear myself a space to sit on the floor and ask Wild if she really could have turned Marei into a frog. She looks at me like I'm 12 years old. "Don't talk silly now, Girl. Whatever gave you that idea?" she tuts. "What do you think we are? Witches?"

About the Author

Paula Hammond is a professional writer based in London. She reads too much and sleeps too little.

*****~~~~~*****

Elf Magic

by Barton Paul Levenson

A small party of elves on horseback approached
The Lodging Place of Travelers in the Uttermost East—a
collection of low-lying buildings at the foot of the Lunas
Mountains. A low wall ran around the outskirts of that
place—not high enough to prevent people falling off, but
enough to let them know of danger. For on its eastern
side, the sky continues down forever.

It was odd, little Alfwine thought, to see clouds
and blue sky *below* one, but like all elfin children he felt
no need to voice his wonder. His eyes only widened as he
rode and saw.

They rode elf-horses, of course: thin and delicate,
more like deer than horses, with long, pointed ears and
tiny horns swirled ivory and indigo over each eye.
Alfwine's father Alfric dismounted first. That was the
signal for the rest of the party. Lord Alfric went in to
negotiate payment with the human keepers of the Place,
and Alfwine's nurse, Folia, lifted Alfwine from his mount.

"May I go see the edge of the world, Folia?"
Alfwine asked.

"I think it unwise. You may play in the meadow,
but come no nearer the edge than a horse-length."

Alfwine nodded his acceptance, and ran to the meadow. Just running and turning cartwheels was enough for a while—a welcome change from riding, sinuous though the beasts' motions were. But eventually acrobatics palled. He noticed an anthill, came near it, and sat down to watch.

"What do you here?" came a voice.

Alfwine looked up to see a girl his own age. She wore an elaborate white dress with puffed shoulders, and the conical hat of a Princess. But her face was brown, not creamy white like Alfwine's, and her ears were round, not pointed like his own. He stood up in surprise. "Are you a human?"

She stamped her foot. "Of course I'm a human. And you are an elf. But what are you *doing* here?"

"Watching the ants."

"Why?"

"To see what they do."

"*They have theyr meat and drink, theyr service and nobilitie, indeed the entire oeconomie of lyfe.*"

"What does that mean?"

"I don't know. I read it in a book."

"What's *oeconomie?*"

"I don't know. I think it means things like a table, and chairs and knives."

"*Ho! Rosalia Infanta!*" came a cry from the adults clustered around The Lodging Place.

"I have to go now," the princess said.

"I'll go with you," Alfwine said.

The two walked up the meadow till they reached the path which wound its way around the buildings. Human and dwarf servants were unpacking supplies and leading horses to outbuildings. "Found a friend, have you, Your Highness?" a man chuckled. A human.

"*¡Hola, Infanta!*" an obese female human cried. She was dressed like Rosalia, save for a wimple instead of the Princess hat. She came up to take Rosalia by the hand.

44

"You have ridden, and you have played, now you must have your nap!"

"¡*Mentira!*" Rosalia wailed. There ensued an impassioned fight in Taraconnensian, the language of the nobility in that country. Finally Rosalia sighed and gave in. "I have to go now," she explained to Alfwine. "You may kiss me goodbye, if you like."

Alfwine stepped forward to do so—and found himself knocked to the ground, out of breath. One of his father's servants had tackled him.

"*Never kiss a human*, you little fool!" the soldier cried.

Alfwine was a moment getting his breath, though the elfin knight was off him and helping him to his feet. "You shouldn't call me a fool," Alfwine said unsteadily. "I'm my father's heir."

There was a commotion among the adults, as Alfwine's father's staff informed their lord what had almost happened.

"Alfwine!" his father called. "Come here!"

Alfwine brushed himself off and went to his father. Lord Alfric knelt in front of his son.

"Yes, Father?"

"Son, your affectionate impulses do you credit. But elves never kiss humans. An elf who kisses a human is no longer an elf. He loses his immortality, and dies in less than a century, to go to whatever strange immortality the humans have. We love you, Alfwine, and want you to stay with us. Because we are immortal, we have children very rarely, and children are precious to us. I must have your word of honor you will never again try to kiss a human."

"I'm sorry!" Alfwine said. He threw his arms around his father and cried.

"There, there. I'm not angry with you."

Later—much later—it was remembered that Alfwine had never given his promise.

. . .

Alfwine, sixteen, bounded up the stairs out of breath, kissed his mother lightly on the cheek, and collapsed on the window seat in her spinning room. Spinning was no hardship for Alfwine's mother, the Lady Ellen. She wove spider webs on her loom into elfin-cloth, light as air, but hard and tough as leather. Elf magic plus cloth of webweave made the wearer invisible in the forest, though the clothes were gay and brilliant in court.

"What cheer have you been having with your friends while I endured this dull magic?" the Lady asked mockingly.

Alfwine smiled. "Hunting and hawking, Mother, hunting and hawking. Mostly the latter. Algar and Elton and I spent the morning in the Forest of the Valley, and Rosalia of Taraconnensia joined us there. Her hawk was always too slow for our elf-hawks, of course, and for a while ours caught all the game we flushed, but then a flight of ducks came by from the river. Well, you know elf-hawks—any loud noise at all makes them shy. But Rosalia's darted right in and caught one of the ducks, third from the right in the Vee they followed, a spectacular fight in the air. And she gave me the duck, Rosalia did! Well, at that, of course, I had to give her all the elf-doves my little Arrow had brought, but it's a fair trade by weight."

"You are still seeing that human?"

Alfwine sat up, his smile gone. "She is a friend, mother."

"And giving you presents quite shamelessly. You were right to respond in kind, that way you owe her nothing. But I think it would be wise of you to avoid her company from now on."

Alfwine smacked a fist down on the seat cushion. "You're always saying what a terrible thing it is for me to see Rosalia. What's so terrible about it? She is gentle and courteous and—and as good as we!"

His mother said quietly, "I do not mean to insult your friend. But humans are notoriously light-headed, and their women are more so. Some day she will ask for a kiss, perhaps not for the first time, and you will unthinkingly give it her, and your immortality will be lost."

"Is that why we hide from humans?"

"*We do not hide from humans!*"

"Is that why elfin castles are always far from human castles? Elfin estates so much smaller, and on poorer land, in forests and never with fields about?"

"We have our preferred places to live, and they have theirs."

"Is human immortality such a terrible thing, that we must flee from it?"

"Human mortality is. You've never seen a corpse, you young fool, save the animals you hunt and hawk. The day you kiss a human is the day you sign a contract to be a corpse some day. To decay, and rot. To be a corpse, and then a mass of corruption, and then a skeleton, and then dust."

"But the soul is immortal."

"It is better to have the body immortal as well."

Alfwine shrugged. "Perhaps if I make this awful bargain I'll regret it. I'll sit watching an hourglass as my last moments drip by, hating myself for doing it and hating Rosalia for making me. Or," and he leaped lightly to his feet and walked almost out of the room, "Perhaps I won't."

"You will. Believe me, if you do this thing you will rue it. *Timor mortis conturbat me*, wrote a human poet. Half their poetry is on death."

"And half is on love, which they deem at least as important, and on which I tend to agree with them."

"Young fool! Do you think I married your father out of love?!"

47

Alfwine slowly answered, "I had always thought it so."

"Well now learn better. His family and mine arranged it. We were brought up better than to let romantic foolishness guide us when it came to so important a decision. We *grew* to love each other. He didn't kiss the first pretty face he ran across."

"How sad."

"And neither will you!"

"We shall see."

"You shall see nothing if you don't learn wisdom from your elders. Look at this!" The Lady Ellen rose from her stool and drew the fine spider-weave from her loom. It sparkled as she waved it through the air. "Do you want all the magic to be gone from your life? Do you want work, and fear, and confusion to be your daily fare? Lose immortality and you lose elf magic as well. Don't do it, Alfwine. Don't throw away your heritage for a pretty face."

Alfwine grew thoughtful. "I suppose you're right," he said.

"Of course I am right."

"But Rosalia is still my friend, and I will not drive her away."

"Then you're a fool!"

. . .

The Feast of Becoming is the most important elfin holiday of the year. Its date varies, found in advance only by soothsaying, but it always falls one year before an event of note in the elfin community—usually a wedding or a birth, though once the start of a terrible war.

Alfwine, now twenty, was Gatekeeper, welcoming his parents' friends and their children and servants. "Lord Aubrey, it is an honor to welcome you to our castle. Lady Ella, you are as radiant as ever. Lord Alfred, Lady Ludella, thank you for coming. Hullo, Alan. And good evening to you, Mistress Elvira! What feast would be complete without your presence?"

The guests collected behind the long table in the Great Hall, filing in on either side of Alfwine's parents.

An out-of-breath servant came rushing up to Alfwine, autumn leaves still clinging to his boots. "Alfwine, someone's been thrown!"

"What? What do you me—"

"By their horse, of course!"

"Well, bring them to the castle!"

"Master, there's a problem." He whispered in Alfwine's ear.

"Find someone to take over for me. Good guests, please excuse me! There seems to be a small emergency. . ."

Alfwine hurried down the path after his servant. Someone called to him from the road, "Ho, young Alfwine! Where are you rushing off to, on this of all nights?"

"Forgive me, Lord Avery! I shall return shortly!"

He entered the forest, hearing behind him, "How precipitate are the young!" followed by "Oh, I don't know. In my fourth century—or was it my fifth? I did something truly foolish."

An unmarked path lay at the bottom of a ravine near the castle. Alfwine saw a horse wandering riderless and a woman limping after it, dresses clumsily hiked up to let her wade through the leaves and stones.

"Rosalia!" Alfwine said.

"Hello, Alfwine, my friend. Could you just catch Dancer there for me?"

"My servant's got your beast," he said as the man did just that. "Take him up to the stables, Elden."

"Sir," the servant said. "Do you think that's wise?"

"I think it's courteous," Alfwine said dryly. "Here, Lady, take my arm. I'll have someone work some elf magic on your ankle."

"You are kind, *amigo*."

"*Y su tambien, amiga*."

By the time they reached the Great Hall, the guests were already bowing as a servant read off their names. "We would seem to have an unexpected visitor," one of the elfin Lords said. "Who is your friend, young Alfwine?"

"If you please, sir: Lady Rosalia de Taraconnensia. You may know that her family fled hither when her dynasty was deposed; she is the true Infanta, however."

Alfwine's father left his place at the head of the table and came around it toward Alfwine. The small amount of quiet background conversation stopped. The elfin Lord's boots clicked on the floorboards.

Lord Alfric stopped in front of his son. "Lady," he said, nodding stiffly to Rosalia. Then, to Alfwine: "You know very well how we feel about this *mésalliance* of yours. Yet you bring her here, on this of all days!"

"Father, her horse threw her! Should I have left her in the ravine—"

"You haven't asked what she was doing out riding by herself, so far from her home, when it is almost dark. Letting friendship blind you is one thing, but letting stupidity blind you is quite another. You will escort her home. Now. And you will not see her again. Ever."

For a long moment Alfwine was silent. "We shall see," he said.

A sharp crack as his father slapped him. "*Ever!*"

Alfwine nodded. "Sir." He turned to the assembled guests. "Lords and Ladies, my apologies. It seems I have an errand to perform."

. . .

They rode in silence through the gathering night.

"Alfwine, I am sorry I got you in trouble. Honestly, I did not plan this. I was out riding in the forest this afternoon and stumbled into a hornet's nest. Dancer

50

took off. I didn't know where I was until I saw your castle."

"I am not angry at you."

"Well, I'm glad." She added, after a while, "Will I never be allowed to see you again?"

"You will see very much of me, Lady. Listen." He reached for Dancer's reins and reined both mounts to a stop. "Listen. My Lady mother says she didn't love my father when they married. It was arranged by their families."

"My Lady mother, she says the same. So?"

"So, one can *learn* to love another. Lady Rosalia—Rosie—could you learn to love me?"

She shook her head. Alfwine looked crestfallen, and then she laughed and said, "No, how could I *learn* to love you when I love you already!"

"Then kiss me." He leaned toward her, but she put out a hand to stop him.

"Alfwine, you must not do this because you are angered at your parents. I know what happens to an elf who kisses a human. I would not do that to you. I would not destroy you—not for anything in the world."

"Would it destroy me to have human immortality?"

"It might. Humans who believe in Our Lord go to Heaven, but those who refuse, to Hell. I would not have you damned for my sake, Alfwine. I would kill myself."

"I won't be. I'll learn human religion from you."

"*¡Ay, madre de Dios!*" She closed her eyes. "Please let this be the right thing!"

They kissed.

. . .

For a while there was silence. Then the traffic noise resumed. A honk behind them. Alvin hit the gas and moved forward. They drove in silence to Rosie's parents' house.

"Let's set a date," Alvin said.

"Honey, you know I want to. But can you live without your Mama and Daddy?"

Alvin shrugged. "I've got a job and an apartment. Look, sooner or later, they'll just have to accept it."

"Honey, you don't think. . . "

He waited for her to finish, but she didn't. "Don't think what?"

"Like maybe we *lost* something when we kissed? Like, then we were kids and now we're grownups, and we can't take it back? I want to do this, honey, I love you so much, but I have to tell you my black ass is *scared*."

He kissed her again. "Don't be. Besides, I have other plans for your black ass." He started fondling her, and she tickled him until he was laughing uncontrollably.

"I was raised Baptist, honey. No whoopee till *after* the ceremony."

"Yeah, right on the reception table."

"You wish. Hey, but really, honey. You won't, like... regret anything? 'Cause you know what we got coming. Your friends asking why you up and married a sinister urban youth such as myself. Mine asking me why I'm living with a white paleface honky cracker. Some fool burn a cross on our lawn, maybe."

Alvin took a deep breath. "We lost something," he said. "Okay, I felt it too. But I'll tell you what: even if there was, I don't know, some kind of *magic* about sticking with your own kind. . . I don't know, maybe there is! You always feel more secure with your own people, right? Safer. You know what to expect."

Rosie nodded.

"But you can't always do it. And you don't need to always do it." He sat up straighter. "I think letting go of that might even be part of growing up. Learning to get along with people other than your own family, and your own ethnic group. Hey, I love you, Rosie. And you love me. And that's what matters here."

She hugged him tight and kissed him again, then let go and opened the car door. "See you Sunday?"

"You bet," he said.

About the Author

Barton Paul Levenson has a degree in physics. Happily married to poet Elizabeth Penrose, he confuses everybody by being both a born-again Christian and a liberal Democrat. He has more than 80 published short stories, poems, and essays. His novels, "Recovering Gretel" and "The Argo Incident," are available from Kindle Direct Publishing. Barton was banned from entering the Confluence Short Story Contest again after winning first prize two years in a row.

Amazon author page:
https://www.amazon.com/Barton-Paul-Levenson/e/B002KDTIMQ/ref=dp_byline_cont_book_1

Home page:
http://BartonLevenson.com

*****~~~~*****

The Sorcerer's Appendix

by Sharon Diane King

The trick *had* to fail, this time. Sieur Peyre had made sure of it. After all, feats of prestidigitation required certain *elements*. Remove an essential one, and—*adeu, Felicia*!

The black-gowned *mestre* took a breath. "Flibbertigibbet, *et quod libet*!"

He leaned over a tall hat upon an oaken table. With a flourish he reached in—

"Oh, not *again*!"

It could not be.

But it was.

Inside the hat, his hand brushed against a struggling creature. Groaning, he seized it, pulling it out by the ears. Long, downy ears. On a full-size rabbit.

Even though he'd gotten rid of the last rabbit he owned.

At midday dinner.

A century later, they might have called him *The Magician In Spite of Himself*.

. . .

Sieur Peyre stood on his stone balcony. Tucked underneath the ruins of an ancient castle, the philosopher's quarters above the Catalan hamlet of Gelida were remote, often chilly, and every year somehow a tighter fit. Yet the view of the town below, set within a lush pine forest, always cheered him.

And of late, Sieur Peyre was in need of cheer.

All of his experiments were failing.

For each *subtractio*—removing an essential part of the sleight-of-hand trick so that it would break—was demonstrating precisely what he was trying *not* to prove.

The manuscript in his hands—a yet-to-be-published tome by his colleague from Toulouse, one J. (for Jean) Prévost—had as its *raison d'estre* that thaumaturgy was not what it purported to be. Magic was not, as popularly conceived, a wicked craft overseen by practitioners of the dark arts. No, magic—the very word was detestable to good Monsieur Prévost—was in truth a rogue's pastime, a motley conglomeration of shams and swindles. It was studied artifice, practiced by golden artists of the fleece, meant to cheat good people out of their hard-earned coin. And it was performable by anyone—given study, a few material items, and the one thing that truly had to be mastered.

Showmanship.

Prévost's manuscript—still with no patron to finance its publication, though replete with dedicatory epistles from bad poets—exposed one magic trick after another. *How to make a knife move without touching it. How to make a rope pass through a man's neck and out again. How to make a vial of water rise up in the air. How to make a coin appear, then disappear, appear again, then melt away.* The volume had tips to pull off its tricks: arranging performances in the shadows, among audiences deep in their cups. Repeating incantatory phrases, using unfamiliar words to befuddle the hearers. Employing callow youths as unknowing accomplices. Alluding to risqué subjects, to draw attention from matters at sleight-of-hand.

Prévost's earnest hope for his tome was to expose the charlatanry beggaring the populace. To set spectators wise.

And—it must be admitted—to make a coin or two himself.

Prévost himself, travelling-bag in hand, had appeared on Sieur Peyre's doorstep some months before. Prévost had pressed his book into the *mestre's* hands, entreating his friend to cross-check his masterwork. Make sure that the tricks worked in the manner described, and only thus. Sieur Peyre could not refuse.

Sieur Peyre had easy success performing the tricks. The trouble began when he started again, leaving out some fundamental element of each trick, to confirm that it was indeed the techniques that mattered. That, well, Magic Was Not Real.

There was only one problem.

It seemed that it was.

. . .

"Your slop jar, sir?"

Sieur Peyre turned from the vellum pages before him to stare at the smudge-faced boy in the doorway.

"Where's your mother, lad?"

"Down with the ague, sir. I'm doin' her rounds today."

The old man pointed. "The Chamberpotted Nautilus is in the corner, *gràcies*."

The boy gazed across the room, taking in shelves overflowing with animal skeletons, glittering crystals, lacquered boxes, glass bottles in which bobbed vague, unhallowed shapes. The youth stumbled past tables littered with pewter pots, globes, scales, funnels, vials bubbling vigorously over candle flames. At length his feet bumped against something solid.

A boulder slowly rose up on sturdy legs. A long neck terminating in a knobby head emerged from beneath a shell.

The creature's deep-set eyes glowered at the boy. It grunted heavily, then trudged off towards the smoky stove.

"Sir?"

"Nothing to worry you, lad. Joan's a bit testy these days. Rutting season, I think."

"*Vale*," the youth muttered, retrieving the covered pail.

"But, lad—" Sieur Peyre interposed. "Could you help me? Watch as I do this trick. Won't take a moment—"

Doubt clouded the boy's features.

"Sit there. Now, you see these three cups on this bench?"

A nod.

"Under this one, I'm placing this stone, spat from the mouth of a demon gnawing on the crags of Montserrat!"

The boy's eyes grew round.

"Not really, lad. I'm just saying that, to make it *sound* impressive."

The eyes grew rounder.

"Keep your eyes on the cup with the stone underneath. *Hic-haec-hoc, huius, huius, huius, huic, huic, huic*!" The cups swirled to the *mestre's* fauxcantations. The youth trembled.

"*Sisplau,* sir—"

"Excellent! You're *supposed* to be affrighted! See how I'm switching the stone in my hand? Now, then! Which cup covers it?"

The boy hesitated, pointed.

"That one, eh?" Sieur Peyre smiled. "You're sure?"

The youth nodded.

As the mestre reached over, the cup next to it hiccupped. It ascended precipitously, stones showering out from beneath. . . .

And underneath it lay the tortoise.

The cups slipped and shattered on the floor; the creature clawed vigorously, trying to get purchase on the polished wood of the table. It raised its cudgel-head and glared.

The boy jumped up, knocking the pail over, and ran shrieking out the door.

Sighing, the *mestre* gently picked up the tortoise and set it outside.

And went for a mop.

. . .

Another day, another trick, another failure.

The accidental mage groaned at each one. He beat his breast, wrung his black cap, swore in all the languages of Iberia. Day and night he pored over the manuscript's detailed explanations, until he thought he would go mad as a rabid badger.

Still, mindful of his pledge, he doggedly kept at the tricks, leaving out one part here, another there, hoping against hope that they would, indeed, fail.

They did not. They kept succeeding, beyond his most fanciful dreams.

And Sieur Peyre would bury his face in his hands.

"I've failed you again, my friend."

. . .

"If you would be so kind, Carme," he told his housekeeper as she hurried in to do the day's chores. "I have a favor. . . "

"Another trick, you say, sir?"

"*Es clar*—"

"No more peas hurling themselves out of the pot, Sieur Peyre? Those quicksilver fumes made me choke!"

"No, no—"

"Or the silly fish, all cooked in paper? What a waste of good oil!"

"No, I assure you. This one should please you. You'll get to lie down!"

59

The woman turned a chary eye on the philosopher, who was rooting through a pile of fake cutlery.

"Nothing untoward, I hope, *mestre*—"

"Not for the world. 'Tis but a harmless diversion."

"*Molt bé*,"' Carme grumbled, clambering into a long box set across two wooden blocks. "But it best not take long. I'll never get the *calamars farcits* for your supper stuffed, and those devilish little squids wouldn't even stay *dead* the last time."

"Now then. 'Ahem. Good evening, *senyores i senyors*. Tonight you shall see the most wondrous feat of legerdemain ever devised! A woman being sawn in half, right before your eyes!'"

It was several hours before Carme's lower half caught up to the good woman's torso, which had been out hoeing industriously in the kitchen garden, so that Sieur Peyre could attempt a reuniting of sorts.

On the upside, however, Carme's chores were completed in half the time.

. . .

It wasn't long before the effects of Sieur Peyre's endeavors began meandering outside his workshop.

For though he had sworn off testing the hat trick, the hat didn't seem to know it. Each time the master reached for the headpiece, he had first to remove its latest furry resident. The hills now ran with hares; his neighbors' gardens stood barren from their predations. Sieur Peyre grew queasy at the very thought of *conill a l'all*, his once-favorite dish of rabbit in garlic sauce. Worse, the hat seemed to be branching out. Heaven only knew where that terrified camelopard had rushed off to, after exiting the hat's silk-lined confines.

In the winding streets of Gelida, tales were whispered of strange happenings. Sections of rope would join themselves together, then uncouple at the worst possible moment—say, when someone was hauling a bucket of water from the well. The wheat in a merchant's bushel-basket would disappear just as a sale was being concluded, then reappear to beguile the next prospective purchaser. Coins used in transactions would evaporate with confounding frequency, leading to miscommunications, mistakes, malaise, and melees. Wine goblets became prank glasses, spilling good Catalan *ull de llebre* all over unsuspecting tavern patrons. Rings of all sorts and sizes would vanish, reappearing in the most unexpected—and inconvenient—of places. The town's tight-lipped barber-surgeon saw his livelihood increase sevenfold in a fortnight.

At last, Sieur Peyre decided that dancing on the end of a trick knife was a fool's errand, and went for help.

. . .

"This way, Father." Sieur Peyre swung wide the front door.

"Segurament." The priest shifted his cassock to clear the last step, crossed the threshold—

—and was instantly enveloped in a vortex of household goods. Chairs hopped upon the floor, a large paella pan banged on the table, fire-filled cups flew about the room. Flip books on the table flashed images of bloody maws full of ragged teeth, as if trying to trap unwary fingers. A broom and a fire-poker were doing a basse-dance of a most lascivious mien. The wide-eyed priest dodged a dagger that flung itself across the apartment, embedding itself in a cupboard.

Sieur Peyre winced. "My last sharp knife. . . "

"Hm," the priest murmured. "Worse than I thought."

"Can you help?"

"Perhaps, my son. After we spoke, I went back through the parish records of the castle."

"But this is not part of Castell Gelida—"

"Not now. But if I'm right, this room is actually the original chapel, set underneath the old keep. During a time of war—perhaps when the crown of Aragon was imposed, woe upon us—they hid relics from the cathedral in a wall recess. They may be the source."

"Relics?"

"They've been known to be the impetus for all manner of, shall we say, *motion events*. Now, if I may—"

The priest began measuring the walls with his forearm.

"Cubits," he murmured. "Thank mercy for that seminary course on cubits."

He prodded the wall, rapping up and down, then nodded at the *mestre*.

"Plastered over. I may have found my niche."

After an hour of poking, prying, and digging with what tools could be persuaded to labor for them—the augur was cooperative, the hammer less so—they discovered a heavy box set in the wall. It took another hour to worry it free. Inside, despite the dust of centuries, enameled containers with Latin inscriptions gleamed.

"The elbow of the blessed Rugiola!" the priest enthused. "The toe unguent of Saint Parsnippus. . . still moist!"

"And pungent." Sieur Peyre's eyes watered. He buried his nose in his sleeve.

"The tie that once held up the breechcloth of the servant of doubting Thomas!"

"*Really?*"

"And a fragment of the timepiece carried by the watchman-saint, Longines!"

The priest closed the box and slipped it back into the wall, murmuring a blessing. He gazed at Sieur Peyre's anxious face, then at the disturbances still suffusing the room.

"I will be candid, my son. I believe these troubles stem from this, er, relic-quarry being the locus of your incantatory activities."

"How can that be? They were mere feats of legerdemain!"

"Yes, my son. But the room—and the transcendent materials within it—did not know that."

"You mean—my tricks *played the room*?"

The priest shot him a glance.

"I would guess this dwelling has long been a space of ESP—Elevated Supernatural Potential, of course. It was beguiled into finding an outlet for it by your skillful hocus-pocus." He shook his head. "Found a place to try its wings, if you will."

Sieur Peyre gulped.

"My only hope now is to—how would your manuscript say? *De-mystificate* this space." He smiled in spite of himself. "Go, my son. Take whatever you cannot replace."

Sieur Peyre tumbled his mother's mother-of-pearl-on-pearl brooch, his father's embossed leather jerkin, and the Prévost manuscript into a sack, and departed.

Seconds later, he raced back inside, grabbed the tortoise, and left again.

The priest opened a small book and solemnly intoned:

"Be it known to all present, I remit this building, and all objects within it, to any secular and lawful use."

He paused, glancing around the room.

*"Also, you've been **had**."*

The otherworld-infused *habitació* may have taken offense at being hoodwinked. Or not.

In any case, it didn't go down without a fight.

From an outcropping down the mountainside, Sieur Peyre—and his shocked shell companion—trembled at the activity swirling above them. The *mestre's* room was now serving as an echo chamber for noises both aethereally sublime and unctuously baneful. Trumpets were sounding. Axes were grinding. Babies cooed. Cows mooed. Pots banged. Ship bells clanged. Chapel, castle, and hill together squealed, rumbled, ululated, belched, as if suffering from a metamorphysical attack of dyspepsia.

The wild sounds reverberated up and down the hillsides, startling Gelidans out into their streets. They stared up in disbelief.

All around the castle, displaced energies in the form of saints, angels, devils, and other minions of the demihallows were vigorously duking it out. The supernatural pugilism raged for hours, though it soon appeared to be more a matter of paranormal rivalry than true antagonism. To this day, Gelidans claim their forebears witnessed blind Saint Lucy using her eye-bedecked platter as a giant fan to shoo away demons. Others witnessed an arrow-strewn Saint Sebastian placidly plucking out the projectiles to distract malingering imps with a game of darts. Crafty Saint Catherine converted her wheel into a proto-unicycle, luring legions back to the infernal realms by having them give her chase. Saint Laurence the Foodie wielded his martyr's gridiron to make a divinely charred, sinfully fragrant *escalivada*.

In the dwindling moments of sunset, creatures of light and dark made up, bid farewell, and quitted the mountainside for their respective dwellings. Peace, like a river, overflowed its banks and swamped Gelida. Citizens began sniping and cheating and carousing of their own free will again. As was only right.

Sieur Peyre ventured up the steps to his workshop, peered inside.

The priest sat slumped on a bench, head in hands. Around the room, candles dimmed, then relit themselves, eggs bounced merrily out of pots, a chicken turned by itself on a spit in the chimney.

Sieur Peyre gently lowered the tortoise to the floor. He grinned.

"Excellent work, Father!"

The priest stared up at him, slack-jawed.

"How in heaven's name can you say that? *Look!*"

He gestured to a pair of gaily-attired dolls dancing a most unconventional version of *sardanes* upon the sideboard.

"But Father! This is nothing but sleight-of-hand. Each time I tried a trick, it turned into something that seemed, well, otherworldly. But these," and the philosopher beamed as he gazed around him, "these all come straight from my friend Joan's manuscript. The jumping egg, the self-lighting candle, the dancing dolls—astonishing frauds, no? Here's another—"

A solid-looking awl appeared in Sieur Peyre's hand. He bowed and promptly impaled his tongue with it.

The priest stared in horror as the *mestre* smilingly removed the tool. A jet of red liquid gushed from his mouth.

"See? I palmed the real awl in my hand for this false one. This is all just—"

The priest flew out the door and down the steps. He did not stop for the shoe that fell off or the cape snagged on a rosemary bush.

"—trumpery," Sieur Peyre muttered. "With watered-down redcurrant jelly for blood."

He sighed, shrugged, and closed the door.

. . .

There was a shuffling behind Sieur Peyre. He stopped threading pages into a cloth-covered book.

The tortoise nudged the *mestre's* calf, bonked its head against his leather shoe.

"I apologize," Sieur Peyre said. "You're quite right, it's supper time." He found the plate of salad, set it down on the floor.

"We'll simply have to find another way of getting you back into shape, Joan. Your human one, that is. I do wish I hadn't begun testing the manuscript with the trick 'To make any creature appear in another guise'. . . "

65

The tortoise stalked off toward the dish and collapsed in a sulk amidst a pile of carrot-tops and lettuce leaves.

"And I should have left you here while the priest was de-thaumaturging the place. I thought it wasn't safe. *Mea maxima culpa*. My poor Joan, or I suppose you'd prefer *Jean*, in your native Toulousain. So far from home, and no way to get you there. . . properly."

The tortoise began making overtures to a ripe strawberry.

"I almost forgot the good news. I received notice in today's post that your manuscript has found a patron. A nobleman of means. He's agreed to pay a publisher in Lyons to see it printed."

The tortoise grunted but did not look up from the plate.

"And I—I hope to write an addendum to your book, Jean. With a caveat to the tricks. First, establish *where* you are to perform them, to avoid. . . complications. Called 'The Sorcerer's Appendix.' Only if you agree, of course."

Sieur Peyre beamed down at his old friend.

. . .

In 1584, a book exposing sleight-of-hand tricks by one J. Prévost was published in Lyons, France.

No appendix was included.

About the Author

Sharon Diane King holds a Ph.D. in Comparative Literature and is an Associate at UCLA's Center for Medieval and Renaissance Studies. Along with scholarly essays, she has had numerous short stories published, including those in anthologies by Dragon's Roost Press and Third Flatiron Press, in *Galaxy's Edge Magazine*, and in the crime 'zine *All Due Respect*. For over thirty years she has directed her own translations of medieval and Renaissance theatrical pieces with her troupe Les Enfans Sans Abri.

*****~~~~~*****

Yin-Yang

by Cayce Osborne

The directions on the *Save Our Seabirds* online forum were cryptic: *Turn off Alligator Alley at the pelican. Find Ernie.* As soon as I got there, I saw what they meant. The pelican statue was carved into the graying stump of a palm tree; its eyes followed me as I passed. A low squawk came from the cardboard box on my passenger seat as the hood of my old Chevy bucked down the gravel road. I put a steadying hand on top of the blanket bundled inside.

At the end of the gravel road sat a slumping salvage heap. But as I neared, the mess resolved into a structure, like a mirage in the desert. Scarred telephone poles were sunk deep into the swampland for support, and drapes of fish netting formed an airy roof. Old highway signs and scrap metal made the walls. Instead of solder or nails, time and salty air had rusted it all together.

My cellphone buzzed, and I glanced down at the screen. Work, probably wanting me to pick up a shift on my day off. I considered it, sense of duty kicking in (*you'll never regret making a little extra money*, my mother's voice advised me, still loud in my head a year after she died). I considered the patchwork dwelling at the end of the road, rolling to a stop. It looked deserted. I shifted the truck into reverse, ready to give up and go home.

Until the cardboard box on the seat shuddered.

"Sorry, sorry, you're right. We came all this way. I'll get out and look around." I tossed my phone into the glove compartment and turned off the ignition, stepping out from the safety of my Chevy.

"Hello?" I said to no one. The sun beat into my skull until my brain felt gooey. "I'm looking for Ernie?" I pulled my long, dark hair off my neck, wishing for an ocean breeze but knowing it was unlikely this far inland.

The place was dead, abandoned. I'd give it five minutes, and then I'd drive back to town and leave the box in front of the Humane Society, even though they'd told me on the phone there was nothing they could do for the injuries I'd described. An abundance of stray dogs, feral cats, abandoned bunnies, and starved horses absorbed their meager resources. And birds died every day: tangled in fishing line, sucked into airplane engines, snapped up by gators or cats.

I retrieved the cardboard box from my truck and began circling the structure, careful to stay away from the edge of swampland, where solid ground dissolved into mush. Two airplane wings—tail number N404BY still boldly printed on their sides—formed an A-frame doorway, invisible from the gravel road. A neat path of crushed seashells led through the center. Claws scraped against the inside of the cardboard, urging me down the path.

The path was lined on either side with airy enclosures, each filled with foliage, pools, and swamp grass. A slash pine grew up through one of them, and a low, throaty *he-he-he* drifted out from behind its needles. A bird, white with vibrant splashes of pink, hunkered on a branch. It eyed me and hopped into the shallow pool on the floor, where it scooped water with a ruined beak.

Footsteps crunched on the shell path behind me, getting closer. A cool breeze brushed the back of my neck.

"Gator did it."

Yin-Yang

I gripped the box tighter, trapping the shriek that had risen into my throat.

"Been trying to re-teach him to forage, but it's been a chore, I'll tell ya."

I turned. A man stood there, stained overalls showing peeks of wrinkled flesh through their gaping sides. His head barely reached my shoulder, and I relaxed. He was so slight, I could've knocked him out with a single breath, like a birthday candle.

"Who'd you bring me?"

"Are you Ernie?"

He nodded.

Balancing the box on one hand, I peeled the blanket back to show him.

"They were doing a controlled burn near Old Marco Junction. Found her under a bush."

"It's a *he*, for starters." Ernie reached into the box and cupped the shivering bird with scarred hands. "Snowy egret." The egret rested his beak on Ernie's fingers and stilled.

Ernie examined the charred white feathers that began at the bird's empty right eye socket and continued to the end of his scorched wing. He was a stark yin and yang: half white, half black.

"Can you help?"

"No promises, but I'll try. I always try."

. . .

I visited Ernie and Yin-Yang every Saturday after that; spending time at the ramshackle bird hospital was a welcome interruption in my litany of *sleep-eat-work* days. Ernie taught the bird to forage with one eye, to hop instead of fly, to find balance in his damaged body. Other birds came and went at Ernie's place, passed on, or were healed and released. Ernie gentled them with hand feedings and encouraging whispers and, I believed, a touch of magic.

71

Next to Yin-Yang, my favorite resident was a grey bird, no bigger than my hand, with glossy black eyes and a broken leg. Each time Ernie passed the enclosure he would pull a harmonica from the front of his overalls and blow a few notes. They were wheezy and tuneless, but the bird cocked its head and trilled the notes back to him. When I closed my eyes, I couldn't tell the difference between the harmonica and the bird.

"How did you learn all this, how to help them and everything?" I asked one day after he'd finished playing for the catbird.

His face darkened, a thundercloud sweeping across a gunmetal sky. He studied his bare feet, tucking the harmonica away. The grey catbird turned tail, flew to the top of its cage.

What had I said?

Ernie gave me the silent treatment until I went home.

The following week, I arrived to find him untangling fishing line from a gull's legs.

"I wasn't a good person, in my life," he announced, not saying hello, or looking up from his task. "This place is my chance, maybe. I think that's. . . " He shook his head. "I'm trying. Undo the bad, learn as I go. Bird by bird."

. . .

I cried the day we let Yin-Yang go. Ernie held the egret as we hiked to the nesting grounds, a nearby pocket of protected land at the edge of Fakahatchee Strand. We set him down, keeping our distance from the nests. Yin-Yang strutted away with unexpected confidence, not looking back.

"They go when they're ready. Not fair to keep 'em cooped. And he's ready."

I nodded but couldn't shake the feeling that Yin-Yang was taking a piece of me with him—a piece I'd just found and wasn't ready to let go of yet. He approached the closest nest, croaking softly. His little bird claws sunk into the peaty soil, and the ghost of them scrabbled against my palms, as they had through the cardboard box the day I brought him to Ernie.

The old man had already turned to go, mind already on the next bird. What a gift of grace, to know when another creature is ready. To be able to let them go.

. . .

I had not planned on returning to the bird sanctuary, but the following Saturday I woke hollow. Missing Yin-Yang and Ernie's gruff charm and the swamp air and the bird chatter.

I drove up the gravel road, waiting for the rickety structure of the bird hospital to appear in the hot air, but it was gone. Not wrecked, but absent. In its place was a deep scar, violently furrowing the swampland. Where the cleave ended, the remains of a seaplane hunkered, its skeletal frame rusted through. The crash site was wrapped in tattered caution tape, its color leeched away by the unforgiving sun.

I parked and walked closer, the body of the plane split open like a mouth gasping for air. Inside, it was filled with sagging stacks of rotting bird cages, littered with feathers. Not the muted colors of Florida seabirds, but much more exotic: red and blue and green and yellow. Tropical birds that didn't belong here.

The nose of the plane was crumpled, its cockpit obliterated. Only the wings were fully intact, tail number bold despite the years: N404BY.

"Oh, Ernie. The plane was yours, wasn't it? This is where you. . . "

I wasn't a good person, in my life, he'd told me. *This place is my chance.*

I looked at the cages, guessing why someone might be transporting a seaplane full of caged tropical birds. If Ernie had spent his life as a poacher and a smuggler as I suspected, and died doing it, he'd made up for it in the after. Saving Yin-Yang and hundreds of birds like him.

"You did it." I whispered into the humid swamp air, hoping wherever Ernie was, he could hear me. I got back in my truck and drove home.

About the Author

Cayce Osborne is a writer and graphic designer from Madison, working in science communication and public engagement at the University of Wisconsin. Her work has appeared in *Exposition Review*, *Typehouse Magazine*, *Defenestration*, *Write Ahead the Future Looms*, *Still Point Arts Quarterly*, and several story anthologies, two from Scribes Divided Publishing and most recently, *Pizza Parties and Poltergeists* from 18thWall Productions. She is the author of four novels. Visit her online at cayceosborne.com.

*****~~~~*****

Shiny Things

by P. A. Cornell

From the moment I first hatched, I've found myself attracted to shiny things. I watched the enormous flying machines land on our world. It was the way they gleamed in the sun that caught my eye. The way they shimmered with color, first blue, then red, then violet. We all watched, those of us in the trees and the sky, those on the ground and in the seas. All save the humans. For them it was never enough to observe. Time didn't teach them the caution it taught us. We held back, surveying this new scene, while the humans resisted.

Where are they now?

New creatures have replaced them. One studies me now, even as I study them. I feign indifference, raising a wing as if to groom myself, but peering through my feathers to observe their reaction. Their scent is unlike anything I or any of the others know. A scent of—elsewhere.

Several of these beings move beneath my tree. I watch them go back and forth with pieces of human-made things. They place them inside something of their own design, then fill smaller objects with what results. I don't pretend to know the intentions of these beings, but if I had to guess, I would say they were unmaking what the humans made. As if you took a nest, and plucked from it each twig, reed, or blade of grass, then broke these down still further into the very things that form *them*.

What purpose do they have for these materials? What's in store for this world now, and is there still a place for us in it? I wonder, do these beings hear the song the trees sing to each other from root to root? Can they smell change on the air, as we do? Humans never could perceive any of these things, though we tried so many times to show them.

My, but they could make so many pretty, shiny things.

The being observing me holds something. Their appendages are arranged like that of humans and other apes. Long upper limbs, useless for flight, tipped with smaller grasping appendages, though many more than humans had. They are delicate. Almost like feathers. They release the thing they're holding, and I watch it hover, rising toward me without a sound. It's round and not much bigger than a grape. I could easily pluck it from the air with my beak, but I stay on my branch and observe.

I lower my wing and watch it gleam in the sunlight. As it approaches, it begins to sing. I *caw* and flap my wings in surprise. My kind are not known for our song, though, so I return to silence and listen. This song reaches within me in a way that's almost physical. It speaks of long transit through stars. Of good intentions shattered. It's a sad song, but one that also carries hope. What happened with the humans—it wasn't what they wanted. It's not what they want for the rest of us. I understand, but this leaves me with questions I'm not sure how to ask.

The being lays the object on the branch next to me, nestled among leaves so that it can't roll away. I understand they mean this to be a gift. I see no harm in accepting it. Later it will join my other shiny things in the place where I hide my treasures.

Shiny Things

I raise my wing again and pluck a single black feather from underneath. I hold it in my beak for a moment and watch the being until I'm sure they understand. Only then do I let it drop. We both watch it float toward the ground, but before it reaches it, they delicately pluck it from the air and raise it to their face to perceive it in whatever way their kind use to understand things. They then take something from their coverings and open it, carefully placing my gift inside.

Likewise, I take the object they gave me and hold it in my beak. I take flight then, leaving the beings far below, and I fly to a place that was once a human dwelling, but that has stood empty for a long time. I add the object to my collection. Then I take a moment to observe the rest of my treasures. A few were found in nature: a seashell, a white stone, the scale from a large fish. But most come from the human world, and I can't help but think of their makers as my gaze falls on a particular object. A child's discarded toy. It's not as shiny as some of my other treasures, but this one is special in that I recognized it for what it was as soon as I saw it. A human being, tiny, but with all its features marked into this hard material. We birds pride ourselves in our nests, so we know skilled craftsmanship when we see it. This piece—it impressed me.

I wonder now about the beings who made it. I can't say I miss their noise, their disruption, their efforts to chase us from places they thought of as theirs alone. But there were kind ones too. Humans who shared food, who *cawed* back in an effort to connect. What of them?

. . .

When I return to observe the new beings the next day, so much has changed. Humans spread through our world, pushing even trees and mountains aside. These beings are reversing it all but at a pace even humans could not have conceived of. Already there is forest where once there was only cold and hardness. Flowers bloom. Streams

77

run where they were once dammed. How could this happen so quickly?

I see a being look up at me and reach a limb into the air. They hold my feather, and by their scent I know they're the one I met before. But I don't yet go to them. First, I fly to an oak and pluck from it an acorn. I bring it to them and think of how it grows into a tree as I lay it on the ground. Does my image reach them?

They approach, and I take a few cautious hops back. But they only take the acorn and observe. They make no threatening move. I smell no danger.

After a moment, they scratch a hole in the ground and bury the acorn. They then step back and begin to sing. I hear a sound like a worm tunneling beneath my feet. Then a small stem rises from the ground. It grows and grows and I see an oak reach into the sky before me. I flap my wings to give it space, and then take flight to reach its highest branches. I watch each leaf unfold as if in welcome. The things these beings can do fill me with wonder, and I *caw*.

The being's song changes, and once again reaches within me so that I understand. They are here to heal this place. I know now that they *are* able to sense the connections between us. I know they want only to connect with us too.

But I still have one lingering question, and so I fly back to my treasures, selecting one. That special one. It's heavier than most; awkward to hold in my beak, but I think it will help me ask what I need to know. I fly it back to where the being is. They are watching for me when I return. I place the object on the ground as I land. I *caw* my question, then cock my head awaiting a response.

The being extends a limb and raises the object, running its delicate appendages over its surface, taking in its shape.

A new song begins, and I feel it like a warm breeze through my feathers. It fills me with a sense of ease. This being has understood my question, and they manage to convey this response: there is hope yet for humanity. They will be raised up once more, like the oak from its seed. They will be returned to this world, but only when it is healed. Only then will they understand and be able to connect with the rest of us.

The being then produces another shiny, round object. It sings to me its desire. I am to share this object with the others—as many as I can reach. It will help spread the word that they are not here to displace us, only to commune and to heal. Should they be welcome, they will stay once their work is complete, but it is our world and therefore our choice. I too have a choice, to take this object—or not.

The object hovers before me, its surface shining in the daylight, and I consider the offer. But in the end, I know what I will do. After all, I've always been attracted to shiny things.

About the Author

P. A. Cornell is a Chilean-Canadian graduate of the Odyssey Writing Workshop. Her short fiction is forthcoming in several magazines and anthologies, including *Cossmass Infinities* and the anthologies *Mixtape: 1986* and *If There's Anyone Left*.

*****~~~~*****

HOPE.

by Emily Dickinson

Hope is the thing with feathers
That perches in the soul,
And sings the tune without the words,
And never stops at all,

And sweetest in the gale is heard;
And sore must be the storm
That could abash the little bird
That kept so many warm.

I've heard it in the chillest land,
And on the strangest sea;
Yet, never, in extremity,
It asked a crumb of me.

*****~~~~~*****

The Black Marble

by Arthur Carey

Joe Morgan looked up as the alien walked into the bar accompanied by a gust of snow. The bartender resumed sprinkling ground nutmeg on a Tom and Jerry for Addie Simpson, who waited patiently. He didn't get to see aliens often, but with the Intergalactic Complex just across the skyway, they dropped in occasionally to experience human culture—or to go slumming.

Joe was a short man with a ruddy complexion and laugh lines under brown eyes that never stopped moving. A worn belt with an outsized cowboy buckle failed to restrain an ample waistline.

"Here you are, babe," he said to the woman. "I'd get on my cell and call a floater soon if I were you. Might take a while to get one in this weather." She nodded and set off carefully toward the sound of laughter, drink in one hand, cane in the other.

The bartender wiped up a wet spot on the bar. Traffic was down in winter, and he was thinking of selling out and moving to Florida. Of course, if the city built that long-promised connector from downtown to the freeway, his business could flourish. If. . .

Joe turned his attention to the newcomer, since only a half dozen customers remained at the end of the bar, nursing drinks, chatting, and scarfing down chips and peanuts.

"Hey, I see the old Star Trek fashions are in style again," he kidded the alien, who eased onto a stool with fluid grace.

"What is Star Trek?" the alien said.

"Well, it's. . . It's an oldie vid show about space exploration," Joe said, taken aback.

The alien, erect and skeletal, towered over the bartender even while sitting. Metallic spangles on its wide-shouldered gray tunic reflected the blinking lights in the mirror behind the bar. Two deeply inset eyes without brows swept over the room. A claw-like hand with seven bony digits brushed snow off a shoulder.

"Pretty cold out there, huh?" Joe said. "Snow in San Francisco at Christmas. Who would have thought? When I was a kid, you had to drive up into the mountains to see snow." He made a circular pass with a cloth, wiping up another wet spot on the bar. "Weather's crazy these days. Heat waves in Alaska, typhoons in the Gulf of Mexico, and Manhattan under water at high tide, just like Venice."

Just inside the door, a robovac crisscrossed the floor, sucking up puddles of melting snow left by the alien. Work completed, it trundled back to its inactive station and powered down.

Joe looked down the bar to see if anyone was signaling for another round of drinks and turned back. "I'm Joe Morgan. Call me Joe. I own the place, which means the bartender never gets paid, but nobody's dipping into the till for themselves." He laughed. "Don't think I've seen you here before."

"No," the alien said. "I am a recent arrival to your world. My designation is Axiatel, but you may address me by my familiar—Axy."

"I don't get many customers from the space complex. Too tough to get here," the bartender said. "Want a Tom and Jerry to warm up, Axy? I just made a fresh batch. The first one is free for newcomers."

He thought about pouring another for himself but decided against it. He'd had several weak ones already. It's hard to be a bartender and not have a drink or two along with the customers.

"Can you prepare an alagonki infusion, formulated with the bruised larva of terososin insecta?" the alien asked.

"Huh! That's a new one on me," Joe said. "Sorry. But I can give you either brandy or vodka in the Tom and Jerry. Okay?"

"O. . . kay."

Joe cocked his head. "Okay, what? Brandy or vodka?"

"Both," the alien replied.

The bartender shook his head. You got to see all kinds running a bar.

He poured the drink, added nutmeg, and placed the glass before the alien. It was downed in one smooth motion.

"Whoa, whoa!" Joe cautioned. "Better slow down, Axy." He brought over a bowl of potato chips.

The alien took a chip and swallowed it. And then another. "This has an exceptionally high concentration of NaCl."

"NaCl?

"That is the chemical reference in your periodic table for sodium chloride," the alien responded.

"Sodium. . . " Joe began, a puzzled look on his face.

"I believe the common term on your planet is salt. On my world, this is a restricted substance. Our younglings are not permitted to ingest it without supervision."

"No kidding," Joe said. "Well, those chips are salty, all right. Makes people drink more. That's the idea." He assembled another Tom and Jerry and pushed it across the bar. The alien took a sip and picked up another potato chip.

"What means 'Last Drop Inn' on your exterior illumination?" the alien asked.

"Huh? Oh, you mean the sign. . . How the bar got its name?" Joe said. "The skyway to Oakland is only a few blocks away, and this is the last bar before leaving town."

"Is this then a refueling facility?"

The bartender rubbed his chin. "Well, I guess you could say that—for some people, anyway. Not much money in it for me, unfortunately."

A high-pitched warbling sounded from outside, once. . . twice. . . three times.

"Your Jet-Go ride's here, Addie," Joe called out.

The elderly woman grasped her purse and cane and hobbled to the door.

When she opened it, a blast of cold air and a flurry of snow greeted her. The robovac darted out, green sensor flashing, and sucked up melting patches of snow that had blown in.

"Hey, Joe! Freshen this, will ya?" A man with a beard waved a glass in the air at the far end of the bar, where a group of people had clustered. Joe picked up a bottle of bourbon and walked down. Returning to his new customer, he noticed all the potato chips had vanished. He refilled he bowl.

"That was Mickey Harrigan," Joe explained. "Mickey's a plastamolder. He makes furniture that conforms to the contours of the user's body when weight changes." He gestured to the gathering he'd just left. "Some of those people are retired, and their families have moved away. Others are new to the city and alone. I keep the bar open on bad weather nights even though there's not much business so they have some place to go where they'll

86

see a familiar face, maybe make a new friend. Big cities can be lonely, ya know?"

The alien belched. Its chest expanded and contracted beneath the tunic, setting the spangles jiggling.

"You okay?" Joe asked. "Want a glass of water?"

"O. . . kay," the alien responded. Joe got a glass of water, and the alien swallowed it.

"Anyway," Joe continued, "I'm thinking of getting out of the bar business. Moving to Florida and sitting on the beach—what beach is left with the ice cap almost melted and the Atlantic Ocean rising like the foam on a beer just poured."

His eyes drifted over the scarred wood floor, from the dartboard and blank vid screen at one end of the room to the restrooms with the faded "Ladies" and "Gents" signs at the other.

"Nobody would buy this place, a run-down bar in a deteriorating neighborhood. No money in it." He shrugged. "Who knows? Maybe people drink more in Florida. I could get another bar."

Joe took another swipe at the bar with his cloth. "I don't know why I'm dumping on you. It's supposed to be the other way around, but I haven't worked up the nerve to tell my customers. So, I'm letting them drink on the house tonight, because they're regulars."

The alien cocked its head. "A house is a surface habitation, is it not? But we are within this habitation, not above it." It fell silent, awaiting an explanation.

"Well, yeah," Joe said. "Saying it's 'on the house' is just an expression. It means free—without charge."

The alien bobbed its head, assessing the information. "Your expressions can have different meanings. That is confusing. Our mode of communication is more precise."

Laughter erupted from the other end of the bar, and they both turned their heads. "These. . . others," the alien asked, "they are of your kindred?"

"Kindred? What do you mean, like in family?" Joe looked surprised. "Nah, they're just customers."

The alien belched again and extracted another potato chip from the bowl. "But you know their familiar signs, and you reminded the one with the appendage support to obtain conveyance." The words came out slightly slurred.

"Addie? The woman with the cane? Sure, I've known her for years." Joe gestured down the bar. "The Kosinskis, Ed and Myrla, used to run a dry-cleaning business a block over. Mickey, the guy whose drink I refilled, lost his wife last year, so he's become a regular to avoid going nuts alone in a tiny apartment. Pete and Ed, the guys arguing about something or other, probably sports, just started coming around. Janie, the woman talking to Mickey, is a prosthesis rehab tech. She comes in here after her shift at the clinic, regular as clockwork."

The alien's head bobbed. "I assimilated in a crèche with many others. I have no idea whose pairing led to my creation. I am a singularity now without kindred, but that will end when I complete my Journey of Discovery and join *The All*."

"Your what?"

"The Journey of Discovery is a ritual passage of growth and study. Before becoming part of *The All*, we must visit other worlds to observe and report on their culture, technology, and social structure. We seek information that may be useful to our own species. Only then, are we admitted to *The All*."

"Yeah? Where are you from, Axy?" Joe asked.

"I am. . . " The alien stopped speaking. It touched a dark line on its tunic and a slit appeared. The alien extracted a black marble. The marble expanded suddenly to the size of a bowling ball and shimmered, catching the colors of the lights over the bar. Joe leaned and saw a reddish globe surrounded by three smaller ones.

"This is my home, Joe," the alien said. "If you hold this and think of yours, you shall see it."

He handed the ball to the bartender, who took it gingerly in cupped hands and gasped. The reddish tint disappeared and was replaced by the familiar image of a blue sphere flecked with shards of green and gray floating in a black void. Joe had seen that before in astronauts' photos taken from space. He was looking at Earth.

Retrieving the ball, which had shrunken to marble size again, the alien deposited it carefully in the slit in its tunic. The slit vanished.

Joe whistled. "That's some gizmo. How does it work?"

"It is a Companion," the alien replied. "Those who pursue the Journey of Discovery and travel far from our world are provided with Companions. When I hold one of my Companions, a neural link is activated. My Companion reads my thoughts and emotions and recaptures images, often forgotten, of things I treasure. It contains my plans and dreams and goals. With it, I am not lonely even though I am alone. I have several of these in case one should be lost or damaged."

The alien looked up at a sprinkling of photos and Christmas cards taped along the bottom of the mirror behind the bar. The photos showed a picnic, a baseball game, and a track with horses.

"What are those?"

"Oh, photos of outings, Axy," Joe said. "I hire a bus—tax deductive—and we go on day trips. Get out of town and escape the crowds and smog. It keeps the customers happy."

"And the other things that look like miniature paintings?"

"Christmas cards. We exchange greeting cards at a special time of the year. Usually when there's snow and cold weather, like tonight."

"Why?"

That stumped the bartender for a moment. "Well. . . to show we like people and value their friendship, I guess. Special times—we call them holidays—kind of bring us together."

"Why do you not express your appreciation directly?"

"Saying how you feel is hard," Joe said, shaking his head. "Buying a greeting card is easier. And we exchange gifts, too."

He plucked a Yule card from the others, stripped off a piece of tape with sticky strips of tape on the back and handed it to the alien. Photographed through a frost-edged window, it showed people holding colorful wrapped objects.

"Ah. . . " The alien's head bobbed knowingly. "Then these cards and gifts are tokens of affinity. You exchange them?"

"Sure," Joe said.

The alien's eyes flicked to other cards stuck to the mirror behind the bar. "Some of the images are different," it observed. "The frozen liquid crystals you call snow, living pods heated by small fires, colorful boxes strewn about a large green plant."

Joe nodded. "Yeah. Snow, fireplaces, and gifts under a Christmas tree."

"These things reflect how you share the spirit of your All." The alien glanced down the bar. "Then those—customers—really are part of your kindred, yes?"

Joe swiveled his head. Myrla Kosinski caught his eye and blew him a kiss before returning to her conversation with Mickey Harrigan and Janie. "Well, if you put it that way, then I guess so," the bartender replied uncertainly.

The alien hiccupped and nodded. "We have similar symbols. They reflect a common bond that reminds us of togetherness and lets us think of good things that might yet be."

The bartender noticed the Tom and Jerry was barely touched, but the potato chip dish was empty again.

A warbling sound penetrated the bar. "I must depart, Joe," the alien said. It rose unsteadily from the stool, one claw clutching the bar for support.

Uh-oh, it's high as a kite, Joe thought, and on potato chips! The salt. . . Gotta be the salt.

"Nice meeting you, Axy, the bartender replied. As the alien turned away, he said, "Hey, wait." He walked over to a rack and pulled off a bag of potato chips. "Here. Promise me you won't eat them now! Save them for later."

The alien took the bag and touched another dark line on its tunic. A wider slit appeared and it thrust the bag inside. "O. . . kay."

A call from the end of the bar drew Joe's attention. This time it was from Pete and Ed, who were arguing again and wanted him to settle a bet about no-grav skitter ball. When he returned, the alien was gone.

But something shiny lay on the bar, a small, gleaming black marble. When Joe picked it up, the marble swelled into a ball. Nestled in his hands, the ball radiated warmth, and a pleasant tingling spread over him. An image appeared. Joe saw himself with Addie, the Kosinskis, Mickey, Janie, Pete, and Ed. They were listening to music played by a male trio in the bar.

He paused. What was it the alien in the Star Trek outfit had said? Something about kindred. That everyone has kindred. He'd never thought about customers that way. Most came and left without making so much as a ripple in his day, let alone in his life. But the others? He glanced at the cards on the mirror.

"What's that, Joe?" A voice startled him. It was Janie.

"Oh, just something a customer left." He covered up the ball, which shrunk in size, and thrust it deep in a pocket. "What can I do for you, gorgeous? Need a refill?"

"Nah, I was just curious. I don't have any plans for New Year's Eve this year. What'll be happening here? Will there be music like last year? That trio of old timers rocked the place."

"Well, I don't know," Joe said. He felt the warmth of the ball in his pocket. "But I'll think of something, Janie. The Last Drop Inn will greet the new year."

She nodded. "Oh, we're running low on pretzels again."

"Coming up," said Joe.

###

About the Author

Arthur Carey wrote his first science fiction tale on an Underwood typewriter rented for $5 while he was still in high school. Since then, his short stories (now produced on an Apple computer) have appeared in magazines in the United States, Canada, the United Kingdom, and Australia. A resident of California, he is the author of *The Gender War* and *Bummer Summer, an Alaskan Misadventure.*

*****~~~~~*****

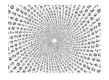

Ephemeralities

by David Cleden

'I am a weak ephemeral creature made of mud and dreams. But I feel all the powers of the universe whirling within me.'
—*Nikos Kazantzakis*

"You mind?" the young woman asked.

Without looking up, I waved at the chair opposite, probably the last vacant seat in the coffee house. Two brim-full cups clattered onto the table, slopping black coffee onto its surface, and I glanced up in irritation.

"Caitlin? *Caitlin*?"

She blanched, clearly unprepared for this chance encounter with an ex-boyfriend. "Dan? Uh—"

"Sit, sit." I scooted my stuff to one side of the little table and eased the vacant chair out for her. She sank onto it gratefully.

"Expecting company?" I nodded at the two coffee cups, but she shook her head.

"So. . . How have you been?"

She looked at me oddly, as though examining my question for hidden traps. "What you really mean is, did therapy help? Yes. For a while, anyway. Then work started to get crazy again."

93

Work. Her work had been the invisible third person in our relationship, the wedge that had finally cleaved us apart. She'd chosen something called the Riemann hypothesis for her post-doc work—a seemingly intractable conjecture in number theory which had baffled the brightest minds down the centuries. I had no real comprehension of it, other than it made some important predictions about the distribution of prime numbers. Like most people, I had a vague idea that prime numbers played a critical part in our interconnected, encrypted lives, but apparently a solution of Riemann's hypothesis would unlock a whole load of other problems in number theory which would come tumbling down like a house of cards. It was the reason it had attracted so much attention over the years, yet had remained unsolved. Typical Caitlin to take on the hardest challenge she could find. When Caitlin lost herself in some inner world of thought, there was no reaching her. She could spend hours—or days—chewing over a research paper she was working on, working on math problems I couldn't begin to comprehend. *It's a limited window of opportunity*, she had told me. Apparently twenty six was the peak age for math prodigies to strut their stuff. By then, your intellect either burned bright like a supernova, or you were already sputtering out in gradual mental decline. How could I compete?

She watched me, waiting for me to say something. Probably wondering if I was still angry with her. I decided to try for something conciliatory.

"You look—" and then like an idiot, the right words just seemed to desert me.

"Like crap?" she supplied helpfully. I nodded slowly. Why deny it? There was a ghostlike pallor to her skin and dark patches around her eyes. She raised a cup in mock salute, took a long pull, and grimaced.

"What's in that?"

"Treble-shot expressos. Two in each cup. I have to stay awake."

"Why?"

She hesitated and then seemed to reach a decision. "I'm forty-eight hours into a sleep deprivation experiment. In another twelve hours, I'll probably start hallucinating. That's when the ephemerality will surface." She took another long sip. "Here's hoping."

"Caitlin—are you in some kind of trouble?"

Our breakup, as breakups go, had been on the whimper end of the scale. No screaming or shouting. No airing of deep-rooted resentments and insecurities, just a slow, painful decay of a relationship, largely through inattention. And I regretted it enough to still care that Caitlin might need my help.

"No, not trouble. Not exactly. It's still there. I know it is. Like a word on the tip of your tongue, or the reason you can't remember why you walked into a room."

"What is?"

She beamed now, and ten years fell away from her haggard face, giving me a glimpse of the bright, eager young mind I dimly remembered.

"I solved it, Dan."

"Solved what?"

She glanced away shyly. "You know what. The thing that's been my obsession for so long. And I solved it."

"That Riemann hypothesis thing? *You solved it?*"

But her momentary flash of ecstasy faded as quickly as it had come. Now she just looked. . . distraught.

"It's gone now. I mean, it's still there—" she tapped the side of her head with a finger, "but I can't get at it."

"I don't understand."

"It came to me in a flash of inspiration, an insight that unlocks the whole problem. It's non-obvious, or I guess it would have been found long ago. But in that

95

instant, I could see it all, see how the pieces of the puzzle fit together. I can't explain how I knew, but I did. It *worked*. It made sense. I was so elated. I remember walking down the university corridors, thinking, *knowing*, this was going to change everything. I had to get some air, so I stepped outside. I don't remember being hit by the cyclist. I came round sitting on the sidewalk, people fussing over me. I wasn't badly hurt, no cuts or bruises, just a bit of a bang on the head where I'd hit the ground."

I leaned forward. "And then?"

"The flash of insight was just. . . gone. It was as though it had dived deep into my subconscious. I tried to recall what I'd been thinking about, what I'd been working on, anything that would trigger the memory—but I couldn't remember enough of the details to recapture it. Since then, I've tried everything I can think of to nudge that flash of insight back out into the open, but it just won't come." She closed her eyes as if in pain. "It's turned into an ephemerality."

"A what?"

"An idea the ancient Greeks had. They used 'ephemerality' to describe some thought or idea too powerful to keep hold of. It was like some creature dwelling in the subconscious. They believed that if an ephemerality were to surface into the conscious mind, it couldn't survive and would soon die. I think that's *exactly* what this is—an idea so powerful my conscious mind can't deal with it. You must have experienced something a bit like it? Some idea or flash of inspiration you struggled to recall later—but you could remember the thought coming to you."

I stared at her. "How can you know for sure?"

"Are you worried I'm a little bit crazy again?"

Huh. Interesting that she'd used the word 'again.' It was certainly a possibility. When it came to smarts, Caitlin wasn't just a level above me, she was somewhere off in the stratosphere. Clever—in that intuitive way that sometimes gets labeled 'genius.' But also. . . unpredictable. I couldn't help wondering if some line had been crossed, that border between genius and delusion.

"A lot of research has been done about what happens when you deprive the brain of sleep," she continued. "Things get thrust up from the deep subconscious. Not always pleasant things. Maybe I can force this ephemerality into the open."

"It's not worth risking your health over."

"*But it is*, Dan. Don't you see? This isn't just a pursuit of personal gratification. Riemann's hypothesis underpins most of the world economy. If we can understand what it tells us about prime number occurrences, it has profound implications for everything from global trade to ordering pizza online."

"All this from depriving yourself of sleep?"

"Putting the body under stress forces the brain to behave in unusual ways. It's how we've evolved. Think about near-death experiences. A person's whole life flashing in front of their eyes in the space of a few seconds."

Caitlin drained her coffee and fixed her bloodshot eyes on me. "Will you help me, Dan?"

Something stirred just beneath the surface of my consciousness; an uneasy thought. Perhaps it was my own ephemerality thrashing like some sea creature from the deep. I should probably get up and walk away. That might be the best help I could offer Caitlin.

I sighed. "Alright. What do you need?"

"I want you to hypnotize me."

. . .

"Phone's recording," Caitlin said. In fact the gently glowing screen was just about the only light in the room, now the apartment blinds were drawn. This wasn't hypnotism in the conventional sense, it was more of a session of deep mindfulness and relaxation. She started the metronome, its *tick-tick-tick* marking out a gentle beat every second, and I cued up the stereo with the soundtrack of rain lashing against rooftops. In the uncertain light, I peered at the sheet of paper Caitlin had given me. It was filled with math expressions I was supposed to read aloud as a kind of priming mechanism for her subconscious. I understood none of it, but didn't need to. My job was to read. And make sure Caitlin didn't doze off.

"This is crazy," I said.

"I know. But there's a lot at stake."

"If this works, are you going to suddenly start spouting math like you're possessed by some kind of Ivy League-educated demon? Will it be like speaking in tongues, or something?"

"I don't *know*, Dan. Maybe all the details will just come floating back to me and everything will be fine. Maybe that flash of insight will surface, and I'll know how to work out the rest of it from there. That's the thing about ephemeralities. They're unpredictable. Fickle."

"You make it sound like it's something living inside you."

"That's exactly how it feels."

I repressed a shudder, remembering far too much time spent watching horror movies.

"Don't let me sleep, Dan. No matter what."

So I sat there on a warm Tuesday afternoon, in the darkened apartment of my ex-girlfriend, listening to artificial rain falling, literally prodding her in the arm every minute or so as she mumbled some kind of precursor math expressions, much like a gymnast warms up before the main event.

I was far from certain this was the right way to be helping Caitlin. I could see how deeply she believed in the idea of ephemeralities—and I wanted to believe too—but if she was delusional, I ought to be getting her a different kind of help. She'd told me this wasn't the first thing she'd tried. She'd popped large doses of Ambien to send her to sleep, setting alarms to wake her every fifteen minutes so she could jot down any dream-like flashes of inspiration. That had gone on for *days*, she'd said. She'd got drunk, got stoned, even hinted she had dabbled in more dangerous substances. For anyone else, that might have sounded like fun times, but the way Caitlin had set about it made it seem very clinical. And. . . creepy?

On every occasion, the ephemerality hadn't shown up, just too shy and timorous to poke its head up into the light of consciousness.

I began to read from the sheet she'd given me, keeping my voice low and monotonic. What else was I supposed to do? Real or not, I could see how deeply obsessed Caitlin had become in pursuing this ephemerality of hers. What else was there left to try? (For an instant, I had the fleeting sensation of something important slipping through my subconscious, elusive and ill-formed. Then it was gone. Dammit—now she had me wondering about ephemeralities. But whatever it was had vanished like a silver fish slipping back into the black depths.)

Thirty minutes later, my throat was sore from reading aloud, and my hand ached from where I kept poking Caitlin to keep her awake.

After a while, I stopped poking and let her sleep.

. . .

Caitlin did a lot of yelling.

After she woke up—sixteen, seventeen hours later, I think—she called me a few choice things. Quite a few. I may have said some things back that I later regretted. When I tried to suggest she seek help from a professional, she told me she'd fix the problem by herself. There was one more thing to try, and she could manage just fine without my further interference.

And that seemed to be that.

. . .

My phone was ringing.

It kept ringing no matter how fervently I wished it would stop. On the second attempt, I grabbed it from the nightstand.

Two forty-four in the morning? Jeez, the building had better be on fire—

"Hello?"

"Dan—?"

Did I recognize that voice? I thought I did, but the memory skittered out of the spotlight of my consciousness. It nagged at me. I did know who this was, if I could just—

"Caitlin?"

"I may've. . . done something. . . a little stupid." Her voice sounded thin, dreamlike. She slurred her words.

"What?"

I was wide awake now, heart pounding in my chest.

She didn't answer. I heard a sound which could have been the phone clattering to the floor, and then. . . A sound like a slow dripping of something onto a hard surface?

"Caitlin? Caitlin!"

I pulled on clothes and ran for the door.

. . .

I thanked whatever gods in the universe were looking down on me that I still had a spare key to her apartment and let myself in.

"Caitlin?"

A table lamp was lit, low wattage, its weak light casting elongated shadows around the room that hindered as much as it helped. It was enough, though, to see Caitlin slumped at the kitchen-diner table, head resting on her arms. She didn't wake.

"What's going on, Caitlin?"

I crossed the tiled floor, but before I reached her, my feet went out from under me. Damn, but the floor was a slippery mess. I twisted as I fell, coming down hard on one knee. There was an ominous splintering sound, and I worried for a moment that I had cracked a knee bone, but then I saw it was only Caitlin's phone, now shattered into pieces.

I pushed myself up, hands and arms slick with the warm stickiness that had spread around Caitlin's chair.

Dear god.

Blood.

I found the wall light switch and flicked it on. A little moan of despair escaped my lips at the scene that greeted me. Caitlin looked as though she was sleeping. I imagined her lowering her head onto her arms as a final wave of tiredness washed over her. But the knife lying next to her lacerated wrist told a different story. It looked as though she had cut more deeply than intended. She would have passed out from blood loss soon after.

I knew what this was about. A thought that had been darting through the pools of my subconscious leapt upwards. *Near death experiences*, Caitlin had said. Shock the body, and the brain behaves in desperate ways, sometimes unleashing a torrent of memories. Not suicide. Not Caitlin. But a deliberate and dangerous dicing with death to flush out her ephemerality.

There was so much blood.

I felt for a pulse, and there was something, but I was terrified by how feeble it was.

She had laid out bandages ready on the table. I grabbed one and made a tourniquet above the wrist laceration, staunching the flow. Caitlin was unresisting; ghostly white.

"Come on, Caitlin. I'm going to get you help."

Something crunched underfoot. I kicked away pieces of Caitlin's phone, then used my own to call the emergency services. They promised to have someone there as soon as they could.

I maneuvred her onto the floor, propping up her legs to keep blood flowing to her brain. She mumbled something. I leant closer.

She said it again, and this time it sounded like, *I remember.*

This was all my fault. If we hadn't rowed, I could have been here to make sure things didn't get out of hand. I could have got her the help she needed. Except, she knew I would only have tried to stop her.

And she'd have been right.

. . .

"Hey."

Her eyes were open, and she was looking at me, but I couldn't read the expression on her face. Caitlin lay very still on the hospital bed, her left wrist heavily bandaged and a drip going into her right.

"The doctor says you'll be fine in a week or two with rest."

Caitlin just kept staring at me.

"Jeez, Caitlin. You nearly died. Nothing is worth—"

"It *is*," She sounded coldly insistent. "We discussed this. It's not just about personal glory. This changes so many things."

"What does?"

"I *remembered*, Dan. In the last few moments before I passed out, the ephemerality came back. I dictated the shape of the logic into my phone. Enough to know how to get back what I've forgotten."

"Your phone." My mouth felt dry. There was a sickness in my stomach, as I remembered the crunch of its destruction underfoot. Her spoken words. . . that elusive ephemerality captured for a short while, only to be lost again.

She took the news well. She probably didn't have the energy to shout at me, and I was grateful for small mercies. But I saw the despair settle over her.

"It's still in there," I told her. "Give yourself time. It will come back, I know it will."

"That's all I can do now. Hope."

I squeezed her hand gently. "Yes."

"But what if it doesn't, Dan? I don't think I can live with knowing there's an answer and not being able to get at it. What if this ephemerality can't ever be drawn out into the light of day?"

"Believe in yourself," I urged her, meaning it. "I do. Really. It's more than just hoping. Call it an ephemerality of my own if you like, but I have an intuition it's going to work out. And soon."

"How can you know for sure?"

I raised an eyebrow. "Isn't that what I said to you? I believe in *you*, Caitlin. Maybe I didn't at first, but I do now." I squeezed her hand again gently. "And this time I'm going to be around to help."

About the Author

Third Flatiron welcomes back David Cleden, who previously appeared in our *Infinite Lives* anthology. Among other credits, he has published stories with *Interzone* and *Deep Magic* and has a story forthcoming in *Analog*.

*****~~~~*****

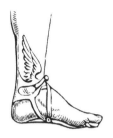

The Ones Who Made the Crossing

by F. T. Berner

All roads lead to Rome, they say, and it must be true. I never meant to come, and yet here I am, longing for the skies of this city, striving to find a place in its alleys, dragging my feet on its old stones, while closing my ears to those stones' songs.

The city is not what it once was, I must say. Before, I just had to wait for the starlings to take to the sky, their murmurations like black ink writing a story on a blue page, and any eyes that turned up would wonder at them, leaving me at liberty to spread my own wings unnoticed. But the starlings are not here anymore, only the endless pigeons and the seagulls, with their shrieking voices and sharp beaks. Seagulls, like rats, will fight a human for a piece of bread—never mind what they would do to the likes of me. So I keep my head down, and I fly very little these days.

I am lucky that people don't seem to notice my wings when I don't fly, nor the way I hobble on talons that I take care to hide inside my shoes. They are too busy to look beyond a nice face and a sweet voice. That's how I was able to land my day job, another insignificant cogwheel in a call center, weaving webs around the ears of old people, luring them into buying whatever I am selling that day. I know I am lucky, luckier that those who have no wings to carry them, luckier than the ones who end up plying their trade on those same streets that led them to the city and never let them leave again.

The call center job pays for the rent of a tiny room and little more, so I work deliveries at night. It's easier lately: more people are placing their orders from the safety of their own home, so there are more shifts to go around, and I get to work every day. Tonight, the first delivery is in a villa, where some kind of party seems to be happening. Music wafts out, along with voices and laughter. The guy who opens the door, in his thirties, is talking to someone inside, and never looks at me once as he picks up the food and hands me an envelope with a tip. I stuff it in my pocket and am out on the street before he can close the door.

The second delivery is for an old man who pores over each item of his order to double and triple check that everything is to his satisfaction. When he finishes his examination, he lifts his eyes to me, his gaze seems to focus, and he slams the door in my face without a word. The third delivery is where it happens.

By contract I am not supposed to go into the buildings, but I still do, especially when the delivery is for one of the top floors. On the way back, if there's no one around, I spread just the tip of my wings and swoop down, savoring that chance for a small flight, a small freedom. The best part is, even if I cross someone, chance is they will just see a person going down the stairs really fast, never noticing, in the badly lit stairwell, that my feet are hovering an inch above the steps. So tonight, on the third delivery, I am anticipating the thrill of the descent, the chance to glide down for eight floors, and while I fiddle with my backpack I don't see the door opening. I only realize that someone is in front of me when I hear a voice calling my name.

"Sandra. . . ?"

After all these years, I should know better than to look a human in the eye, and a man at that. But the surprise at hearing my name spoken aloud is such that my head jerks up, and I find myself looking into his eyes, those brown eyes with the deep shadows that still haunt the dreams I don't dare to dream.

. . .

I met him many years ago, somewhere on the Ionian Sea. He was sailing the Greek islands with some friends on a summer vacation. My sisters and me, we were on a different kind of journey. The smugglers had towed us offshore, then cut the rope and left us there, with no oars and no rudder, in the middle of the sea in the darkest hour of the night.

We knew this would happen. The smugglers never made the Crossing themselves, they just towed the boats for the first stretch and then went back to shore, leaving passengers to their luck. Many sank to their death, an offering to the Gods of the depths. Others were stranded in that desert of salt water until the blazing sun scorched them, and they died of thirst. Still others were spat back to the shore, sometimes after a long ordeal where they were chased by sharks, and then they had to find a way, and the strength, to try again. Only the lucky few would be picked up by a current and carried to the other side.

Before that night, we had already crossed mountains and deserts, suffered hunger and war, and we had fought our way through. And we knew that after that night there were still more hurdles to overcome, unimaginable ordeals and hardened gatekeepers to block the way to paradise. But that night was our Crossing, the threshold to another world, the whole reason for our journey.

107

There, in the darkness, waiting for our fate, I felt one of my sisters shiver next to me. It was Sylvia, the youngest, still almost a baby. I groped around, until I found her hand and squeezed it, but soon I realized that the others were also beginning to waver, so I did the only thing I could do to keep their hope alive.

I began to sing.

It was a song from the Old Country, as old as the Earth's own bones. Its words were lost to time, blurred through the voices of mothers and brides and crones, interspersed in the melody of lullabies and wedding songs and lamentations. And still every living creature that heard the tune would know it in their heart and be able to sing. My sisters soon joined in, one after the other, Sabina's deep alto like a steady undercurrent, the twins with an unadorned melody in perfect unison, Shayla and Sarah's voices chasing each other around the highest notes.

That's how they found us, Uli and his friends. They followed the music.

. . .

I know I am three times luckier than most. I left the Old Country, escaping the knives that killed our parents. I made the Crossing, and while a current didn't pick up our boat, Uli himself was the current that ferried us across. And here, at the end of the road, at the end of all roads, I found a job, a job that keeps a roof over my head and food in my belly, though the roof is just a room below road level and the food is whatever is on sale just before its expiration date.

Others are not so lucky. Even my sisters, who escaped with me, who crossed over with me. Sylvia they took away before they even let us set foot on land, because she was so young. On good days I hope she's been adopted to a nice family, but good days are few and far between. Soraya went to fetch water one night at the refugee camp, and after that she never spoke a word again; they found her drowned in a tank a few days after. Selina fled during the great fire—we all did, but while many of us went back, her I never saw again.

I am thinking about my luck (I don't need the deliveries, I tell myself; I have a day job), when I see my boss Laura's name blink on my phone. I only do deliveries for her at night, so if she calls in the morning, something is wrong, and today there is only one reason she may be calling.

"Do you have anything you want to tell me?" she asks as soon as the call connects. Not even a hello. It doesn't bode well.

"I don't know, Laura. Is something the matter?"

"A client called, asking about you."

Let it be the old guy, let it be the old guy, I plead in my mind, as if repeating it could make it true.

"What did he say?"

"Aha! So you know it was a man!"

Why is it that humans always seem to gloat when they think they got you? As if they had something to prove. I have learned that there is only one thing to do: try and make myself inconspicuous. I bathe my voice in deference and hide behind a web of feigned ignorance.

"I only delivered to male clients yesterday, Laura. What did he want?"

"You know there are plenty of people ready to take your place. I don't want any problems."

"And you won't have any from me, I promise," I tell her, adding another touch of sweetness to my voice to hide the fact that it is trembling, that my whole body is trembling. *What did he say, Laura? What did he want?* But she has already disconnected.

I swipe my badge and run to my workstation. I am a couple of minutes late because of Laura's call, and the line manager shoots me a look that feels like it could burn me to the ground. It's probably the first time he has ever noticed me. I keep my head down and try not to look in his direction as I connect the first call of the day—but my voice is feeble, charred, worn out, and for the first time in years I don't close the sale. I don't close one sale for the whole day, and each time the manager looks in my direction, his gaze is a little more focused, a little more pointed. I may need the deliveries more than I thought, after all. I stay a bit longer at the end of the shift, to make up for the lost minutes, but I know it may not be enough.

Or rather, I don't know. Not knowing is the worst part. Not knowing if I still have ground beneath my feet, if my wings are still strong enough to fly, not knowing whether my card will be declined, or whether I will still have a room to stay in after the end of the month.

I rush to the restaurant to take up my deliveries, but across the road I stop in my tracks. He is there. He sits at one of the tables on the sidewalk, turning a spoon around in his coffee cup, though the cup is empty, the coffee already drunk. He toys with the spoon absentmindedly, while his eyes scan the people who pass by, looking for me.

Before I can turn around he sees me, before I can run away he is already in front of me.

"Sandra."

My name, again. Since I lost my sisters, no one has spoken my name like he does now: not as a handle, but like a complex story, a story he weaves himself into. And suddenly there's no ground beneath my feet, only the rising and falling of waves, as if my Crossing had never ended. Because maybe it never did.

. . .

He was not the strongest of them. The others, those who did not want to take us on board, could have bound him to the mast and sailed away, leaving us to our fate.

"What if they are sick?" whispered one of his friends. "Who knows what illnesses their kind may bring!"

"They are too many, there is not enough space on board," said another.

110

"They will take control of the yacht, and throw us all overboard," feared a third.

"Don't be silly," Uli retorted. "Don't you see how scared they are? We *have* to bring them to safety. And how would they take control, anyway?"

"With a spell," went on the other, his eyes wide open. "Like that song they were singing, that was clearly a spell. I say we leave them here and go back."

And yet, that's not what happened that night. Uli talked to them, in his quiet voice, and soon we were on board. At first, I didn't know how he had done it: he didn't scream and impose his will by force, as did most men I had known before. He didn't cajole them lacing his voice with honey, like I do with my call center clients. His voice wasn't even sweet, but rather gruff, as if he had smoked too much too soon, or screamed his freedom and his joy into the wind for too long while surfing the waves. And yet his friends, they couldn't help but listen to him; they would have had to plug their ears with beeswax not to.

Later that night, as we were sailing towards a safe haven, with my sisters and I huddled on the bow of the yacht, and his friends still eyeing us with distrust, Uli made hot tea and came to sit next to me. He asked if we needed anything. And then, gently, he asked me about our journey, our life. I was hesitant at first, but talking with him was easy while the darkness of the sea gave way to the first light of a new day in a new world, so I told him about the Old World. Not everything, of course, just sparks of the truth, the colors, the mountains, the old songs, but also the knives and the terrors, and the dangers of the Crossing. And when he asked, I told him my name.

He, in turn, told me of his life, of his girlfriend Penny, back home, and their hope for a brighter and better future, of how they had met at a human rights march. And when he spoke my name, that night, in the middle of the sea, he was making me part of their story, as if spreading their warmth, and health, and happiness, to cover me and my sisters and the whole world.

. . .

He speaks my name, and again I am. I am no longer alone, I am no longer unknown or a stranger. I am seen.

It is scary to feel seen again. In this city, in this new world, I have learned to disappear: I cloak myself in darkness, don't look anyone in the eye, don't fight, not even against the seagulls, just so that the gaze of these people sweeps over me without focusing, just so I can be safe. I take comfort in the short moments when I can glide on the tip of my wings, when no one is looking. And I have plugged my own ears with beeswax, so as not to hear the old stones of this city sing their stories that are older than this world.

But when Uli speaks my name, I am again part of a story. Now he is introducing someone—his *wife*—and a brown-haired woman I have never seen before is hugging me like a long-lost sister. She smells like well-brewed coffee, but her hug is light as feathers and reminds me of the Old Country, of honey-colored light, of the crimson taste of pomegranates, and mint wafting through the air. Of home.

And for the first time in years, I don't hide. I don't run. I feel seen, but also welcomed. For the first time in years, I am again part of a story: a story from the Old Days, like a bell tolling under the waters of a lake, a story that is father and mother and husband and wife, a story that is roots and mountains and hearts and skies. A story that every living creature would know in their heart, because it is their story, too.

###

About the Author

F. T. Berner has always loved weaving words together, in many languages, so she became a translator and then a writer. She lives in Italy with her husband and loves the city of Rome—though she has yet to spot a winged siren there. "The Ones Who Made the Crossing" is her first professional story. You can find her online at ftberner.wordpress.com.

*****\~\~\~\~\~*****

Vanishing Act

by Raluca Balasa

When I say I am becoming invisible, they laugh and reply, *But I can see you. You're right here.*

My therapist nods like a bobblehead and brings out the sing-song voice that sets my teeth on edge. *And what makes you feel invisible, Zora?*

I get it. When they look at me, they see a small-boned, frizzy-haired girl with freckles dusting her nose and eyes set too deep, too far apart. Straight out of Psych 101, they think, the unremarkable often feel ignored. Have I tried pole dancing to boost my confidence? Reciting positive reaffirmations in the mirror? Dating more?

But my last date looked right through me when I greeted him. Would have *walked* right through me, too, if I hadn't jumped out of the way. He veered for the bar and struck up a conversation with the bartender. I caught the words *stood up* and *hard being a straight man these days* before deciding I'd dodged a bullet.

Or, if the bullet, too, had gone straight through me, at least I hadn't felt it.

. . .

The first strange incident happened a month ago at work.

Working at the Toronto General Hospital means washing your hands ten, twenty, fifty times a day. I can't count the number of times I've scolded grieving wives and parents for going straight from the crapper to the door. You can open hospital doors with your foot these days, not that anyone ever does. No, people wrap their piss-stained fingers around the door handle and continue with their lives feeling good about themselves.

"Aren't you forgetting something?" I said to an old lady wearing a knitted skirt. Scolding old people feels worst, but it comes with the job. Nurses deal with all the crap—literal and figurative—that doctors don't want to handle.

Now, this woman *did* notice me. She turned back, frowning, and ran her hands under the faucet as if they were butterfly wings too delicate to thoroughly wet. Still not a great washing technique, but she'd tried, so I held my tongue. While she ripped paper from the automatic dispenser, I moved to the sink to follow my own advice. The first faucet—the one Grandma had used—didn't work, so I tried the second. The third. Fourth.

I looked up then. I'm not sure why—maybe I wanted to share an exasperated glance with myself—but I caught my reflection *flickering*. Only for a moment, like the wink of sunlight on glass, but in that brief moment, I had disappeared.

Finally, my eyes moved beyond my now-steady reflection to the old lady's behind me. She didn't seem shocked or surprised. In fact, she was watching me with tight lips curling, as if she enjoyed seeing me fail my own test. Right: I had piss-stained fingers to resolve. I moved my hands fast, then slowly, but not a single faucet worked. Sweat pooled beneath my scrubs.

Muttering curses, I dug through my purse for my champagne-scented sanitizer. I spilled some onto my pants, but the paper towel dispenser wouldn't cooperate, either. The old lady left the bathroom shaking her head and muttering, *"Sacre bleu, quelles manières horribles..."*

. . .

I've never seen my reflection flicker again, but maybe that was when I started fading. Maybe that little old lady had cursed me for calling her out on poor hygiene.

At first, I didn't think much of it. Easy not to notice you're fading when you come from a long line of Sicilian Italians; you can hardly get in a word anyway. I rent a one-bedroom in Scarborough, but my parents and grandmother live in Barrie, so every other weekend I'd return to (a) report what I'd been eating, (b) confirm that yes, I was still single, and no, my priority at the TGH was *not* snagging a young doctor, and (c) help with whichever crazy projects my family had dreamt up that week. Most recently, Dad had decided to build a fence. Only *stupid Canadians* consulted instructional YouTube videos, so I had to do it myself while he hammered posts at roughly seventy-degree angles from the ground.

"Listen to me, Zora. I know how you think. I used to be just like you."

"Have you even measured the perim—?"

"You need to start a family. Your best years are already behind you. Desmond has a son about your age—a little dull, but maybe you'll like him."

You have to understand that Dad never means these comments as insults, which drives me even crazier. The road to hell is paved with good intentions or however that saying goes. "You're not doing it right," I snapped. "The video says the posts need to be every six to eight feet—"

"Look at your Ma and me. Huh? Where would we be without each other?"

117

At which point Ma stuck her head out the window and shouted, "*Che uomo inutile!* Does that look like a fence to you, *Nonnina*?"

And *Nonnina* was happy to take it from there.

I don't have siblings. My only cousin lives in Germany. Often, I wished I was more invisible to my family. If they didn't want to hear me, why did they have to see everything I did, to judge the way I had chosen to live my life? Why couldn't they just fully ignore me?

Nonnina would say I am paying for a sin against God—that by wishing this, I've incurred His wrath. Or perhaps she would shush me and wrap me in her arms, and I would sit in her lap like a child as she braids my hair with ribbons and tells me tales of old Sicily. I can no longer know. I have passed out of existence, while my grandmother—my family—remains solid and unmovable as stone.

. . .

If this *is* my fault, I must have racked up the bad karma. The thought eats at me in my lowest moments. Do I deserve this? I've never been religious, but if there is a god out there, I'd like to see an inventory of my sins. Maybe that very thought is one of the sins that landed me here.

But there's something else, a deeper sin, if you would call it that, that sits hollow in my gut, even in those moments when I ascend above self pity—something I regret for the act itself, not because it might have led me to invisibility. Let me tell you about a recent patient of mine.

His name is Mr. Jankowski, and he pretends he doesn't speak English, so that the nurses call his grandchildren to translate. He's constantly in and out for palpitations and high BP. Typical stuff. Wife died a year ago, which I think catalyzed his need for attention.

"Ignore him," says Grandkid Jankowski. "Tell him you'll give him more meds and send him home."

118

Vanishing Act

What a bitch, I thought the first time her grandfather came in. I skipped lunch to play Scrabble with him, though he kept pretending not to know any words except *cat, bat,* and the like, so the game was rather unsuccessful.

She exaggerates, I thought the third time Mr. Jankowski came in. I spoke with Dr. Nussbaum to switch him from Norvasc to Metoprolol and start him on Lorazepam for anxiety.

He is *a little irritating,* I thought the seventh time Mr. Jankowski came in (BP 180/80). His English got miraculously better every time I saw him and every time Grandkid Jankowski refused to pick up her phone. I started suspecting he came in just to see me. To talk to someone.

"You're neglecting your other patients," Dr. Nussbaum told me. "There are people here who actually need your attention."

So I began ignoring Mr. Jankowski. Cut him off when he went on his *I-gave-up-a-scholarship-to-the-University-of-Warsaw-for-my-kids* tirade and refused to return his smiles in the halls. Something inside me broke, then, seeing the effect that had on him. His face melted like candlewax.

He hasn't returned to the ER since. I don't know what happened to him, but I think about him every time I am stared through and my shouts—for attention, validation, a little bit of affection and human contact—go unheard.

. . .

I became invisible on an exponential curve: slowly, then so fast I could barely process what was happening. At first, it was only technology refusing to respond to me, which seemed inconvenient but not overly odd. Technology's always screwing up, right?

Soon, though, I had to say something five times before getting a response—not just with family, but at

119

work. Patients didn't notice me taking their vital signs until I squeezed the pressure cuff around their arms. I signed in for my shifts and spent countless hours at the TGH only to have the other nurses swear they hadn't seen me all day. I grew tempted to see if I could actually move *through* people, so I tried it one day. Instead of swerving in the hall to avoid a collision like I normally did (men never moved first, but lately, not even *children* had been giving me the right of way), I held my ground. Banged head-on into a visiting cardiologist. He dropped his clipboard, papers swirling slow-motion into the air, his glasses askew and the stethoscope around his neck hanging like a crooked tie. Poor man looked absolutely befuddled. He muttered a quick apology, but I could tell that I hadn't left an impression on him. As he bent to pick up his papers, he muttered, "Must have been mopped. Damned janitors didn't leave a sign."

It was another week before I thought to reframe my invisibility as *invis-ability*. Hokey, I know, but how else was I supposed to get through this? Here was my chance to learn all the stuff nurses weren't supposed to know.

So, on a busy Wednesday afternoon, I loitered in the reception room listening to two neurosurgeons gossiping, hoping to overhear something about a promotion or raise. Turns out neurosurgeons' gossip is just as dull as the receptionists'. Dr. Nussbaum had a crush on Jenny (who didn't?), the OR was in for a remodel, and Dr. Muller was expecting. Big deal. I was turning to leave— standing right in the open doorway, I *still* hadn't been noticed—when I heard my name.

"What about that loud Italian nurse? Zora something?"

Loud? I chewed the inside of my cheek and flipped him off, but, of course, he didn't react.

"Haven't seen her in weeks. She on rotation?"

"No idea. Have Mindy check her work records."

And that was it. No one said my name again in the following weeks, and then it disappeared from the sign-in sheet as if I'd never been.

. . .

Today, I haunt the hospital: a true ghost.

I've stopped seeing my therapist; it wasn't helping, and eventually even she stopped seeing me. I can make myself noticed if I shove people like I did with that cardiologist, but they squint and stare as if they can't quite piece me into a whole. When I called Ma last week, all she heard was static.

Have I considered becoming a thief, you ask? A master assassin? All plausible employment options. Maybe one day I'll pursue them, but for now, I can't bring myself to leave the TGH.

Not yet. There are people here who still need my attention.

An old woman sits in a wheelchair on the seventh floor, forgotten with her hospital gown backwards and half open. She doesn't seem alarmed when I kneel and start buttoning it for her. It's clear she needs a bath, so I wheel her to her room and start prattling on about the latest season of *Vikings*. Her milky eyes roam the ceiling while I talk. I know she doesn't see me there, but for the first time in months, I don't care. Dirty water sluices off her, and eventually she cracks a relieved smile.

All of it evidence that I still exist. There's no way to know if I'll lose my ability to act on the physical world, but I try not to think about that. One step at a time. For now, I take comfort in the methodical, circular motions of sponge on paper-wrinkled skin.

When the nurse finally arrives, he finds the woman clean and settled into bed for the night. "Vikings," she says when he takes out the menu and asks what she wants for dinner. "It's not just that everyone's hot. There's a great plot too."

. . .

I might no longer be seen, but on some level, in some plane, I am heard. While this knowledge doesn't help with the loneliness, it gives me purpose. I became a nurse because I wanted to make a difference, but nursing is more than a degree and the title my family is so proud of. Now, for the first time in my life, I understand what my job truly entails.

When I visit my parents in Barrie, I see that they have forgotten me. *Nonnina* still hums my name in a sing-song way, then gazes into the distance and whispers *quale poesia?* wondering whether she's heard it before in a poem. In the kitchen, Ma stirs a pot of soup, pauses, tastes, and says, "Something's missing." We both know she is not talking about the soup.

I go to the backyard to stand beside my father and whisper. The fence will be crooked. Take out the posts and start again. It's alright to admit that you were wrong.

"Nothin' for it. Gotta take out the damn posts," he mutters.

Ma sticks her head out the window and hollers that she hasn't asked him to un-make a goddamn fence. What kind of a man can't even build a fence? Silently, invisibly, I make my way back inside to her. Try positive reinforcement. Let's be honest, Ma: you're no *Nonnina* in the kitchen, yet he's never had anything but praise for your work.

Her face softens; I can see beads of sweat at her temples and fog on her glasses from staring down into the soup. She looks out the window again, stirring contemplatively. She does not go out to him, but she doesn't shout again either. With Ma, you have to take the small wins.

I keep to my regular schedule. Work, home, family visits. It takes me two weeks of rifling through computers and files at the TGH to find Mr. Jankowski's contact information. Now, I sit in my living room with a glass of pinot—stolen from the Liquor Control Board store, since I

122

figured I deserve *something* good from all this—and dial Grandkid Jankowski.

"Hello?"

"Call your grandfather."

"Uh. . . hello?"

"He gave up a lot for you and your mom, you know. Could have gone to the University of Warsaw on a full scholarship. Did he tell you that? Don't be a bitch, so call him."

"Damned scammers," is all I hear before she hangs up. I do this for two more days until she blocks my number. Then I start calling from the hospital.

I have no way of learning what's become of Mr. Jankowski. But Ma smiles at my father now, and the fence stands straight and tall in the backyard.

About the Author

Raluca Balasa holds an MFA in Creative Writing: Fiction from the University of Nevada, Reno. Her approach to writing is character oriented, often dealing with love/hate relationships, antiheroes, and antagonists who make you agree with them. Her short work has appeared in *Andromeda Spaceways Magazine, Aurealis, The Mithila Review,* and *Grimdark Magazine,* among others.

Currently, Raluca works as a freelance editor and English teacher in the Toronto area. Her debut science fiction novel, *Blood State,* was released in September of 2020 from Renaissance Press. She can be found at https://ralucabalasa.wixsite.com/website

*****~~~~~*****

Stella

by Melissa Mead

Nell watched the falling snow muffle the buried outlines of parked cars. Nothing moved, not even a bus or taxi. For once, the city was quiet, and looked clean.

When at last the snow stopped, she stepped out onto the front stoop in her bathrobe, breathing the cold, clear air. If the neighbors saw, they'd think she'd lost it. Mrs. Johnson would probably call the police again. But out here, if she closed her eyes, she could pretend she was standing in her backyard at home, and that the snow was falling on stubbled fields. At least until she looked up. Instead of stars peeking through dissipating clouds, she saw the smoldering orange tint of sodium lamps.

She sighed, becoming aware of the cold, and turned to go back inside.

"N-nell?" said a faint voice.

She looked across the street. A little figure stared back at her, dark against the snow.

"Who are you? What are you doing out in this weather?"

The child-sized shape struggled toward her. Nell waded into the snow-covered street, scooped up the trembling stranger, and carried her inside.

Once they were both safely indoors, Nell got her first good look at the child, and gasped. The girl- or at least, it seemed like a little girl- wore nothing but her own long, straight hair. Jet black. So was the rest of her- not black like people are, but ink-black and faintly shiny from head to toe, even her lips and palms. Only the whites of her eyes differed, and even those looked slightly luminous. Nell stared for a moment, then wrapped a thick, warm afghan around the shivering child.

"I found you!" the girl said through chattering teeth. "I didn't think I would, because you've been in this blind spot so long. But I did!" She looked Nell over thoughtfully. "You're a lot bigger than I remember."

Nell searched her memories, sure that this strange-looking girl would have stood out. "I'm sorry. I don't remember ever seeing you before."

"Well, I was home then, and it's really far away. And I can't see you from there now, because the air's so dirty. But I could hear your heart. Why don't you talk to me anymore?"

"I. . . I'm afraid I don't remember talking to you either."

The child looked about to cry. "But you named me! You used to come outside with the looking-thing, so you could see me. You said I was your star, and you named me Stella, so we'd rhyme. And you'd wish on me. I didn't have wishes to give yet. I SO wanted to give you yours! You were the only one who wished just on me, every time. You never got what you wished for, but you were my friend anyway. And now it's my first Wish Giving Time. I wanted to give my first wish to you, but you weren't there anymore."

Nell put a hand on the child's forehead. It felt normal. No sign of fever. "Where are your parents, sweetheart?"

She giggled. "Stars don't have parents, silly!"

"Wait. You're saying that you ARE a star?"

126

"Yes! I'm YOUR star, from when you were little. I just told you. I've got my light inside so I could come see you. But it's awfully itchy. I don't think I can stay long. Can I give you your wish now?"

"A wish? For anything?" It was sweet that this strange child wanted to give her a wish. The least she could do was play along.

"Yes!" The little girl—Stella—cupped her hands and pressed them to her heart.

"Hold out your hands."

Nell did, and gasped when Stella poured silvery light into them. Her hands tingled.

A vision flooded her mind. Her childhood home, a dark shape in the starlight. The scent of fresh-cut alfalfa from the nearby farm where her father helped with the milking. Cicadas shrilling in the grass.

"That's where you used to talk to me!" Stella exclaimed. "You'd stand right there, next to that big rock." Awash in memory, Nell didn't ask how she knew.

"I loved that house," she murmured. "But the farm went under. My dad lost his job, so we had to move to the city."

"But now you can wish to go back! And stay there forever and ever!"

Nell returned to herself, blinked, and looked at her hands, faintly shining. "I really could."

"Yes! And you could bring the looking-thing, and we could talk together."

Someone knocked on the door. Nell opened it, and found a youngish policeman on the step. He looked familiar.

"Hello again, officer!" she said, positioning herself in the doorway. "Another call from Mrs. Johnson?"

His apologetic look confirmed her suspicions. "Sorry to trouble you at this hour, ma'am. We've had a report of a lost child."

"I'm not lost!" Stella piped up from the couch. "I ALWAYS know where I am!"

The policeman gave Nell a questioning look. She sighed inwardly, stepped aside, and filled him in on the believable aspects of what happened. ". . . and with the roads this bad, I didn't want to risk taking her out. She seems healthy."

The officer was nodding, looking less concerned.

"You forgot to tell him I'm a star," said Stella.

The officer gave Nell a Look. "We'd better take her over to Medical and get her checked out."

Nell swallowed some uncomplimentary comments about nosey neighbors. "Stella, this gentleman wants to have a doctor look at you, to make sure you aren't sick from the cold."

"I NEVER get sick. And I need to stay until you make your wish."

"Wish? Happy birthday?" said the policeman.

"Not exactly. Could we both ride with you? I think she'd be pretty upset otherwise."

"Are we going to ride horses?" Stella looked thrilled.

"No, we'll ride in a car." At the policeman's slow nod, Nell scooped Stella up and pulled the afghan more closely about her, praying that he wouldn't notice just how unusual his passenger was.

Throughout the slow, slippery trip to the hospital, Stella pressed her nose to the window in rapt awe.

"Look! Is that a cat? Are there birds? I'd like to see birds up close. So many lights! No wonder I can't see you here. I'd use my next wish to open a window we can see through, only you'll use yours to go home, so you won't need it."

Stella held Nell's hand throughout the trip and into the ER, where her exuberance dimmed.

"It doesn't smell right in here. And people are crying."

128

"I know. Some of them are hurt. But they come here so people can help them get better."

Stella let a nurse put an ID bracelet on her wrist and sat, tense and trembling, on a paper-covered table.

"I'll need to start an IV," said the nurse. "She's probably dehydrated."

"What's an IV?" Stella asked, wide-eyed and wary.

"We need to put a little tube in your arm, so we can give you medicine. It won't hurt much, Sweetie," said the nurse. "Just a little stick."

"You—want to make a hole in me?"

"Very tiny. And you can pick your favorite Band-Aid to put over it afterward."

"No, please don't! The light will come out, and I won't be able to put it back!"

"Can't we skip the IV?" said Nell.

"Sorry, no. We might need quick venous access."

"Please don't!"

"Sorry, Sweetie. I'll be quick."

"I really don't think we should. . . "

The needle went in. Stella didn't scream or cry, just shut her eyes tight, her face contorted with strain.

At first, Nell didn't see anything different. Then she noticed that the faint shimmer around Stella was visible, even in the bright indoor light.

"I'm sorry," Stella whispered. "Please go away quick. I'm TRYING, but it hurts."

The nurse stared. Starlight bled around the needle. Stella opened her eyes. They shone hot blue-white.

"Please," said Stella, weeping starlight. "I don't want to hurt anybody."

Nell reached for her, but Stella shrank away, radiating heat. Everyone was staring now. Some backed away, but not fast enough. The paper shield on the table began to smolder.

"Nell! Please hurry. I'll open the window next time. I promise!" Stella clasped her hands over her heart.

Nell understood. She repeated the gesture and shouted for the heavens to hear: "I wish that you were safe at home!"

Starlight flared one last time.

. . .

Eventually, after rounds of explanations and cross-examinations that didn't really satisfy anyone, Nell came back to her apartment. By then the snow had melted, but the night sky was still gray and orange, and starless.

Stella had promised to open a window, next time.

When would "next time?" be? Decades? Centuries?

Crazy to hope that a little girl could open a window to the stars.

Ridiculous to believe that she'd talked to "her star."

Nell stood on her front porch, searching the opaque sky for a certain point of light. She shook her head, went back inside, and dug out the jar that held her "Someday Savings." Time to buy a new telescope. If. . . no, WHEN Stella opened the window, Nell would be ready.

About the Author

Melissa Mead's publication credits include *Cast of Wonders, Intergalactic Medicine Show*, and *Daily Science Fiction.*

*****~~~~~*****

Yes, Sadly

by Nicholas Stillman

Palmer didn't know anymore how far the foliage surrounding his house went. He had to try another glance at the world, and standing just outside his door gave him no better vantage than any of his windows. The huge bungalow still felt more like a shell he could wait in, a temptingly roomy one even with all its prepper supplies. Its previous two owners stood nearby, one of them an oak and the other an elm. He suspected a divorce had occurred, as most couples in the area had turned themselves into matching firs. He watched the lowest boughs of each pair swish in the wind, still touching at the tips like lovers who held hands.

He looked at the nearby houses where things just sat forever inside. Outside, the yards quickly became a forest. He spotted entire new trees the Earth had never grown before. He longed for real neighbors, human ones made by God. Time just wouldn't kill his memories of them.

Mattison joined him outside, bringing all her scruples with her. Two years ago, her eyes could lift the sunken spirits of a whole room. Now, she had a dour face for the day set in already. Palmer felt reassured anyway just by seeing her perfect build. In her old, close-fitting work coveralls, she looked almost naked sometimes. Nothing wild grew out of her except her hair, and in the gentle wind, God did what he wanted with it.

Palmer glanced at the name tag sewn onto her uniform and shuddered. She still looked saddened just by wearing it, like a woman watered down by so many labor jobs seemingly drawn from a deck of cards. He could see the same loneliness in her soul that he felt, the same desperate need for community and belonging. His own name tag still declared him a research assistant of the lowest rank. He had a whole life planned out that never happened.

"Promise me again you won't go near the city," Mattison said without even trying to wake up. "A whole building could fall on our heads."

"I really never planned on it, hon," Palmer replied. "We'll find someone out here. We won't have to go far."

Palmer sidled through the yard, dodging every branch that reached for him. Mattison walked with him like a shadow. The driveway of the property they had taken over only led to more abominations: people turned into bushes, cacti, and perennial flowers. The regular vices had held them down before, but now their plant bodies kept them rooted. Their leaves did their dances in the sunlight, but through no human volition. They had strange stems and petals that could survive the full pain of winter.

The road sounded so quiet Palmer presumed he could eat off it. His own footsteps sounded too loud for him. He walked around the lower plants, the former people who could not afford the bigger, fancier transformations. He saw whole communities of them grown in clusters as the economy had wended down. The advent of the biotechnology had forced nearly everyone to become plants as entire industries and livelihoods phased out. Palmer gazed at the inexorable result: the plant pills had put the whole world on a beanbag chair. The shrubs, once children, crowded out the natural tallgrass. Even the weeds lay dead and rotting, unable to compete with such comparatively fast mutation rates.

As he stepped off the unavoidable moss, it sprang back up by design—human design. He couldn't help but wave to it at least once. The plants did, after all, have some odd, undetectable sentience. Mattison only raised an arm to cling to him, her hand like a creature on his shoulder. They witnessed the ultimate sloth made possible. All the new species luxuriated as the summers and winters fought it out forever above them. Their leaves rustled as though greedy for more easy solar energy. The wind picked up and stirred every high branch, pulling off a few leaves. It seemed God already contested their goal to remain sated and sessile for eternity.

Palmer and Mattison moved like athletes. They climbed a hill while listening for any new chorus of man-made sounds. At the crest, they found only foliage burgeoning everywhere, like a new fuzz for the world. They saw weird, gnarled trees, like soldiers dominating the highest hilltops. From the nowhere behind them to the nothingness ahead, they found everything green and serene—and horrifying. What they once called humanity now sprawled before them like fixed tapeworms siphoning from the Earth. Palmer noticed clothes strewn about like meaningless letters written on the moss. They all looked long-abandoned and mostly covered in dead leaves.

"Do you still think. . . " Palmer began.

"Yes, sadly," Mattison replied. "No one called or came over. The remnants of the internet stopped working for us months ago. Who could resist the temptation to go totally sessile? They've also got that druglike steady euphoria. Even you once called it a new high for the masses to try on."

They went onward, down the hill and up another one. They found countless varieties of new plants which satisfied the human need for individual expression. Some trees touched at the branches, while others only mingled at their roots. Instead of nations, scores of the same species displayed their solidarity of thought and ideology.

"Maybe God will forgive them," Palmer said. "Think of their primitivism as a sort of antiwar effort. Plant warfare, if it ever happens with them, wouldn't hurt as much as human war. They've even abolished pollution."

Mattison found a smirk from somewhere. "How did you get so smart?"

"Breastfeeding and more breastfeeding. Before that, a pretty good time in the womb. Don't worry. We'll find a few of the strong and faithful."

Palmer smiled while looking afar, but Mattison's face said something akin to *no*.

They ventured on but found nothing that moved in the world but boughs in the breeze. Higher trees flaunted the status of the upper classes, gushing out their leaves for summertime. The tall, contorted trunks, once human, boasted a higher kind of treason. They defied God's image of man as much as possible.

"Not everyone would have taken the pills," Palmer said with a wave to no one. "Can you imagine a whole population of decadents versus God? God will win regardless of the collective's immense knowledge."

Mattison stopped and pointed. "At least some of them still sympathize with us boring old walkers."

Palmer followed her finger to a bunch of grapes growing from the tangled verdure. Every cluster grew at the same eerie height—the height of the average human hand that may reach for them. He walked over and picked one. Like the moss, the stems would perceive such contact as a free massage, a stimulation to dwell on for decades.

"We'll have to eat these when our supplies run out," Palmer said. "These altruistic types will feel pretty euphoric about it, too. They sense what we do to them, but

I think God will add the real pressure. Someday, all their sentience might evolve down to nothing."

Palmer took a test bite. He felt something akin to his ancestors telling him not to, but it would spare his girlfriend from having to instead. His mouth filled with little fireworks of sweet flavor.

Mattison's eyebrows bent downward for the rest of the day.

"Not a trace of human DNA remains in these," Palmer said. "They went all the way, hon, the farthest from God they could possibly go. But you know him. He's forgiven our defiance before, countless times."

Mattison turned, but in doing so she spotted something far more haunting. Beyond the trees ahead, a stagnant little pond produced only slimy green bubbles. She looked like she wanted to hop away a few feet despite her distance from the scum. It resembled the same kind of algae her whole family had changed into. Reeds grew around it as well, just like the ones Palmer's parents had become. Even the bushier life around the pond equated to death, at least socially.

Before Palmer could comfort her, *he* jumped back a few feet. A lurking bear poked its muzzle from the bushes right before him, startling both himself and Mattison. The grizzly, released from a zoo or lab, only went after the grapes. Its ears didn't even flick as the couple fled by instinct.

Palmer huffed and nearly giggled at their overreaction. The docile bear, like every other beast, hardly noticed them after generations of domestication. Mattison, however, held that same annoying look of aversion and solemnity as always. Her eyes crystal-gazed into all other objects but him. He could tell she sensed an eventual danger from such animals, and her mouth became just another stress meter on her face.

"Come on, hon," he said. "They have shrunken amygdalae from all that selective breeding. It'll take generations to develop fear and cunning again, *if* God allows it."

They walked until the multifarious plant forms piqued her into talking again. She pointed at something sick and floppy. "Weird. What did they even call this one?"

"A fern, I believe. They call those parts the fronds. I call it just another ugly head on the behemoth."

"And this ropy one?" She pointed higher.

"A vie-yan, I think. No, a *vine.*"

"Vine. Hmm. Like those grype or grape things."

"Look. See those specks under the ferns? They release what they call spores into the wind, millions of them."

"Spores. . . derived from seed?"

"Likely, hon. Imagine the bliss of having countless offspring."

Mattison scoffed. "Bliss? More like greed."

"More like gluttony, too."

"No one can resist so much."

Palmer threw his best smile at her. "You and I did. Come on."

They pushed through the bushes only when they had to. The world had too many poor folk before the pills had come along. Mattison's face remained locked in scrutiny—until they both noticed a human leg.

It lay on the leaves, naked and pale. The rest of the man hid behind the verdure. Palmer and Mattison hurried around the big bushes and gazed at their discovery: an abhorrent puddle of a man, someone who looked more like a jellyfish plopped on land. Only one other appendage had not yet liquefied into a pluripotent slime. Something protruded from the jellied limb—maybe a branch, maybe a bone. He had real bones, somewhere. Though reduced, they still held up the central mass which slowly wriggled like a half-crushed spider. Parts in the center had already turned translucent green with speckles of advanced chlorophyll. The greeny bits spread like sand in a slow wind. A half-melted face drifted about, with a lump for a brain shriveled to almost nothing. The organs at the bottom had sprouted rootlets, with most of them already subsumed by the ground.

Mattison squinted until her whole face gave up. Palmer held back a series of grimaces. The man's clothes lay nearby like a collapsed ghost of someone. The pile included a hat which had the dust beaten off it too many times. The pants looked faded, dirty, and broken in by the countryside. The shirt looked like it had given up on everything too, like its wearer. He had only recently taken the pill to start up the whole metamorphosis.

Mattison trembled. "What. . . what will he become?"

"A lost soul in hell," Palmer said without looking up. "Let's go."

He allowed himself one shudder. His legs wanted to do something about the whole mess, so he let them. He and Mattison walked away. As they trekked toward the city, their shoulders always touched.

"Darn," Palmer said. "So close to our house."

"It wouldn't have mattered." Mattison had that knowing gaze again. "He had temptation in his heart. They do what they do, and they all do drugs."

"Maybe not. Maybe he felt the same desperate loneliness that we feel. We have to reach down and hoist them up, hon."

"You mean reach up?"

She gazed at the treetops. Palmer warped his face into a smile and hoped it would spread to her. Mattison, however, gave him bad looks and darker forecasts.

They climbed a final hill that overlooked the city. Palmer's heart hammered like it wanted out of him. He hurried, surefooted and staring, pulled to the mere idea of a few moving vehicles. Mattison followed, staring at nothing along the way.

"We spent too many days in our own little prison," Palmer declared in a huff. "We can't let the world roll by without us. I won't hide in disgust forever."

They reached the hilltop, and Mattison's hair moved like fire in the wind. They beheld an overgrown cityscape, a toy humanity had abandoned. Only plants lived there, saturated in sin, the purest sin possible. Ivy had taken whole buildings, the brickwork beneath it already thickened with moss. The skyscrapers looked more like tall, fuzzy hills with their lofty gardens rounding out the rooftops. Bushes ruled over acres of parking lots, and any trace of pavement had long since vanished under new soil.

Palmer witnessed a world no longer knotted up with highways and power lines but with creepers just as long. He beheld a mere spot on that world like any other. The truth of the apostasy fell on top of him. All of humanity had gone away like the dreams he had as a boy. He and Mattison stood perfectly, divinely alone.

"I guess we don't need surnames anymore," Palmer said, his eyes hot with tears.

He tore off his name tag and threw it in the wind. Mattison tore off hers. She looked naked again and unfathomably special without it. Truth gleamed off her somehow, more than ever before.

She talked mostly to the sky. "I feel like he'll speak to us soon. We'll get instructions so people may walk on this Earth again."

Palmer faced her. "What? Really?"

"Yes."

"Well, you've felt your way to the right places before. Just look at us, still human despite all this pressure. Gosh, hon, I wish you would tell me the moment you feel something like that."

"Alright. I love you, Adam."

"And I you, Eve."

###

Yes, Sadly

About the Author

Nicholas Stillman writes science fiction with medical themes. His work has appeared in *Total Quality Reading*, *Zooscape*, *The Colored Lens*, *Bards and Sages Quarterly*, *The Martian Wave*, and *Polar Borealis*.

*****~~~~~*****

The Wonders of Yesterday

by Shannon Brady

"You," said Macak, hopping up onto the arm of Niko's chair, "are entirely hopeless."

"And *that,*" Niko shot back, "is incredibly big talk for somebody with four paws and no opposable thumbs. I'd like to see you do better!"

In response, Macak gave him a long and supercilious purr, tail swishing as he appraised the sleek silvery laptop on his human's knees. The narrow metallic headset loosely strapped to the side of his head glinted in the sunlight coming in through the window, and the row of tiny indicator lights glittered a cheerful green up and down its edge.

"Well, for a start, I think you should try using *your* oh-so-superior fingers to get out of the downloads page?" he suggested. "That isn't where the actual programs go."

"But the installation wizard said that that was where it was—"

"No, you *downloaded* it, but that isn't where it went. Go to the desktop menu, that's where the actual icon you need to select is."

"How would you know? You're a cat!"

Macak nearly spit, luminous yellow eyes narrowing. "Excuse you, I was right there doing the whole thing alongside you. It's not *my* fault that my laptop isn't the working one, or else I'd go ahead and show you."

He momentarily stopped swishing his tail to incline it towards the cardboard replica of Niko's laptop lying on the coffee table, constructed and fairly well painted by Niko's daughter Estelle. The only downside to receiving it as a Christmas present, Macak had decided, was that he had not been there to stick his paws into the artistic process as it was happening. Pleasant surprises were pleasant and all, but. . . paints and brushes. *Paw prints.*

Niko, meanwhile, was busy making the customary Disgruntled Old Man Noises as he tapped at the touchpad. "Okay, I think I got it. . . wait a minute—since when did I need a username and password to get into Caelestis?!"

"You—actually, I'll give you a pass on that one, Sterling basically made the company account for you."

The sleek black cat hopped off the arm of the chair and set about searching through the box of index cards in the TV stand, pawing through them until he found the one that contained the access codes. With the aid of the headset, expressing his thoughts verbally, in human language, had been a surprisingly easy skill for him to pick up. Niko had been saying, with his usual begrudging affection, ever since Macak was a kitten that he was a very intelligent cat.

Making sense of their writing, however, was another beast entirely, and he had to admit that he hadn't quite gotten the hang of it yet. However, with close inspection, he *was* able to recognize the word "Caelestis." He counted himself very lucky that Niko had such large and neat handwriting.

Once he was sure he had the right index card, Macak picked it out delicately in his teeth and trotted back up to the chair. He hopped up onto the other arm and dropped it onto Niko's lap, as if it were a dead mouse from the backyard. "There. Recognize any of this?"

"Hrmph." Niko adjusted his glasses. Of course, there were better treatments and high-tech contacts available to him nowadays, as Estelle and Sterling kept reminding him, but he'd been wearing these for decades and had no intention of changing now... He peered at the card. "Yep, looks like you got it. I don't know *why* Sterling wouldn't let me use the same things I usually do. I keep saying, if you change up the letters and numbers just a little every time, it's perfectly fine."

"If you say so. You're the human, after all. Oh, that's a lowercase L, not a number one."

Niko grumbled unintelligibly as he backspaced and then typed in the correct characters. "There, how's that look, smart guy?"

The small speaker on Macak's headset crackled softly with feedback, as he gave a long, amused purr. "It looks to be in order. Go ahead and hit Enter."

With a grunt of assent, Niko did. The login screen for Caelestis's communications network, as casual as it was meant to be, was designed in a way that neither human nor feline particularly liked. Estelle called it *professional* or *minimalistic,* but what Niko and Macak both thought but did not voice was *intimidating.* The screen was solid black, with no background, icons, or artwork of any sort, save for the corporation logo at the top of the page, which was done in a bold, striking sapphire font. There was nothing else except the access code entry, and once that was input, the login bars disappeared, only to be replaced by a deep blue loading icon, swirling on the pitch-black background. It made Niko think quite uncomfortably of a black hole. There weren't even any stars to add a little light and optimism to the image.

Strictly speaking, Niko didn't interact much with social media, outside of keeping up with his earthly relatives and posting all the pictures of Macak that the cat insisted upon, but even he recognized that they were much more welcoming than this. Among the choices that Caelestis made that Niko disliked—that *worried* him, somewhere deep in his gut—this was probably the most minor. But still, there was a reason that the phrase "straw that broke the camel's back" had been coined.

Niko startled at the sudden sensation of a rough, wet nose nudging at his fingers.

"You need to quit being so tense," said Macak, as he pushed his way under his human's hand. "Unnecessary stress is just *terrible* for your old bones."

"Hmph. Been doing some reading, have you?"

"No, I just listened in on your phone calls with Estelle. Before we had to go through all this trouble just to talk with her, and all of them. I suppose I should thank you for putting her on speaker all the time."

"It's a habit. It's why I never minded all that video chatting stuff when it came out: I could just prop the phone up or put the computer on the table, and we just could talk like normal. It was almost as good as face to face."

"Mm, if you say so. I've always thought that it just isn't *right* without somebody's scent to go with it. Or a lap to lay in, or scritches behind the ears," Macak added, angling his head to get Niko's idly petting fingers in just the right spot by the base of his left ear. "But this is still pretty interesting, I have to admit."

"That's one word for it." Niko watched the loading icon, still leisurely swirling on his screen, and his bushy eyebrows furrowed. "Should it be taking this long to connect? I swear, *nineties* Internet was faster than this."

"You should expect to be giving it a while, shouldn't you? They're all a *little* farther away than the next county over, you know."

144

"Yes, I *know,* Macak, thank you." Niko sighed, not even bothering to disguise it as a huff. For a moment, his gaze roved out through his sliding door, to the sun just beginning to set over his small backyard, and the faint white imprint of the moon ready to rise against the deepening colors of the sky. "It's not as if I wish she made a different choice. I think sometimes she gets that impression from me."

Macak purred. "She knows how you feel. Anyone can see that."

"I'm sure, but I don't. . . I don't want her to think I'm disappointed with *her.* Or her decisions, really. I don't like why everything seems to have to *change* nowadays; it doesn't have to be different to be good, and I don't get why nobody else seems to understand that."

"I understand. I've always lived a rather static life, headset or no."

"I remember when Ralph's grandson got accepted into the trainee program. That kid is so happy. But can Ralph be happy with him? No! All he can do is be spiteful about how now he won't be around to clean his garage and shovel his show and all that crap. Like he doesn't get to have his own life. The last thing I want is for Estelle to think I didn't want her to go. She's been so happy ever since she got the position with Caelestis. But still. . . "

Macak glanced up at his human, and thought that if he had that sort of mouth, now might be the time when he would give a knowing smile. "I'm sure she misses you too, Niko."

Niko's face did a complicated thing, but before he could get his thoughts together, the program made an accepting *ding* noise, and the blue swirl was replaced by a video screen with Caelestis' logo. Macak's ears perked straight up.

"Look alive, old man! We're on!"

Niko had exactly one second to banish any conflicted thoughts and get his game face on, before the connection was fully made, and the image of a very different living room blinked onto the screen. Filling the camera were four faces grinning from ear to ear: Estelle, her husband Sterling, and their daughters Skye and Lucina, ages twelve and ten. The latter two squealed excitedly when Niko and Macak appeared clear as day on screen, but it was Estelle's voice, high-pitched with delight, that drowned everything else out.

"Dad!"

And just like that, Niko didn't have to fake a smile at all. Happiness shone out of every line of his beaming face. "Honey! How're you guys doing?"

"Grandpa, we're in space!" Lucina shouted, waving her arms wildly.

Niko laughed heartily. "I see that!"

"Hi, Grandpa! Hi, Macak!" Skye waved one hand more calmly, but her eyes looked brighter than ever. "We're good up here, how's it going back on Earth?"

Macak let out a loud, open-mouthed meow, his speaker crackling. "It's a lot more homey, that's for sure. What's all that behind you, a movie set?"

Skye laughed. "Come on, Macak, you know it looks cool!"

"Yes, freezingly so. And I'd bet we've got much better food here than you've got up at Caelestis Station."

"You eat *cat food!*" was Lucina's rebuttal. "Even the powdery stuff we've got up here has gotta be better than that!"

Macak licked his paws primly. "Oh, I beg to differ."

"You look well, Estelle," Niko was saying, while Macak continued to debate the girls on the pros and cons of space and Earth. "Your work's all going well?"

"Lots of gases and rocks and cosmic sound waves," Estelle replied with a shrug. "It's all been pretty typical so far, but there's never been a particularly slow moment. There was a dust storm on the planet's surface a

146

few sols ago, and we all got to watch it from one of the observation windows instead of just on a screen!"

"Sounds *wonderful,* hon."

Niko had been an accountant for forty-five years before retiring, and while he was far from unintelligent, he had never kept up with the sciences outside of finance and economics. So ever since Estelle and her interests were young, he had often found it difficult to keep up with the astrophysics and biological sciences that she talked about with ever-increasing fervor. Still, he liked to think—and to remind his grandchildren—that "difficult" should not mean "stopping point," and he had always tried his best to take as much of it in as possible.

He figured he had to have done something right. After all, his daughter had never once hesitated or held back in talking to him about her passions, and it remained his favorite thing in the world to listen to.

Of course, as most full family conversations did after some time, the subjects changed one after the other. Sterling's engineering work was a bit more of a challenge now that they were actually aboard the station, the girls were still getting used to the schooling program, and *The Martian* had been shown as the weekend movie screening, much to everyone's amusement. Niko, having had more time to read since retiring, told Estelle about the books he'd finally completed, and hastily took down several more titles on an index card when all four started recommending them to him. The discussion between Macak and the girls about the games the three of them had played at home versus the entertainment available on the station bobbed up and down through it all.

And while some part of Niko was unsure whether he'd really be able to keep it—he wasn't *that* old, and he'd always been hale and hearty, but still—he promised that, however long they stayed up there, he would throw them a huge welcome-home party when they finally returned to Earth. Macak meowed loudly in agreement.

It was pleasing, if nothing else, and ended up being a fitting close to the conversation; it was fully dark now here on Earth, and while they experienced time differently up there, it was important for all four of them to maintain a proper sleep schedule on Caelestis Station. It did not escape either Niko or Macak's notice that the goodbyes lasted a fair bit longer than they did when the family was leaving their house, or calling them normally on the phone. Macak wondered privately whether they were thinking about it as well.

There was no hard and fast limit on video calls from Caelestis to Earth, so rather than the call timing out on its own, Estelle had to physically click the "end call" button with a final "Bye, Dad!" The screen blinked instantly back into blackness, and it almost gave Niko a jolt. He was suddenly hyperaware of the empty weight of the machine on his lap, the heat coming off the bottom nearly burning his knees.

That last image of all four of them waving goodbye to him was imprinted in the front of Niko's mind. He did not like to feel it quickly turning fainter: so many of the details of his family slipping away like water. Another second, and tears might have begun to sting his eyes, but a low and thoughtful purr from Macak distracted him.

The cat, for his part, had left his lap and was crossing the room to stand at the sliding door to the backyard, gazing with no small interest in the night sky. The full moon was looming large and golden, the stars endless points of white brilliance around it.

"Niko, can we see Mars from here?"

"Yeah. It's very close to us."

"What should I look for?"

"Look high, up in the southeast sky. There should be a little red to it."

Macak mewed assent. He lifted his head higher and focused harder, as if on the hunt for prey. "I think I see it. But I'm not sure: it's so tiny. I don't think it's close at all."

"I guess it depends on how you look at it." Niko's voice was determinedly steady. "They're going to make great changes one day, aren't they? All four of them."

"I'd say they already are, going up and away where no humans have been before and all."

"Even greater than that. Like nothing anyone on this planet has ever thought of before. They'll...they'll make the most amazing things so common they're downright boring. They'll change the whole *galaxy.*"

"Oh, I'm sure. I'm just a cat, after all, I don't have anywhere near as high aspirations as you humans do. Whatever happens, I'm sure I'll be shocked."

"I'm proud of them, you know? And I'm glad. Even if they never come back home. . . " Niko took a long pause, and Macak politely did not look back as he swallowed hard, several times. "It'll be a good thing, I'll say that however many times I need to. I'll be *proud.*"

Macak purred. "They know, Niko. And so do I. I'm looking forward to it all, too."

His human really was never quite as hopeless as he thought.

About the Author

Shannon Brady is a fiction writer who lives in New York with her family. She graduated cum laude from Purchase College and holds a Bachelor of Arts in Creative Writing.

Her previous works can be found in such publications as Queer Sci Fi, Jerry Jazz Musician, and Dark Peninsula Press. When not writing, she can be found baking, reading, and looking for new movies to watch.

*****~~~~*****

Final Report from the Land of Red-Headed Children

by Bonnie McCune

We live in a neighborhood that no longer exists. That's strange here on Earth, because these people believe only in information gained with physical senses, and the neighborhood definitely exhibits tangible qualities. Its residents decided to eradicate all indications of the neighborhood's presence when they discovered it was named after a discredited leader. They thought changing the name would void its existence from life and remove the stigma of shame.

They failed to understand the past always exists, trailing like ghosts after corporeal beings.

To change the name, three popular elections were held. The first two elections confirmed the neighborhood's old name. When leaders refused to accept the will of the people, self-appointed superiors launched a third poll. That one finally delivered the death blow by approving the elimination of all traces of the old community's name on signs, in directories, online, and removing maps and internet references from the face of the Earth.

The supposed nonexistence of the area matters not at all to me and my peer pilot. As humans say, "A rose by any other name would smell as sweet." We knew the area continued its being, regardless of its label. We were determined to stay, as we sought a rare resource that we had reason to believe exists on Earth.

The planet captivated us from touchdown, before we even knew any of the *homo sapiens* names. We exited our shuttles, which were curved and round like eggs, disguised to fit into the surroundings in what natives call "earth tones." When each individual shuttle split for our egress, left behind were hemispheres, rough to the touch, appealing to the eye, statuelike, resembling works of art we'd seen on our viewers for weeks.

The reason for our caution in approaching the world was the reputation of Earth, known for its raging, virulent viruses as well as its biological variety and beauty. Another reason for caution—the primitive extremes of its dominant species. We'd been warned by our researchers that *homo sapiens* retain indigenous reactions. They are quick to love and equally quick to violence. Our working theory is they are relatively early in their evolution. A scan of their communications indicates their genetic manipulations and improvements continue to fall into the "primitive" category, so the inhabitants still must suffer under the challenges of unbridled instincts rather than the rational mind. The behavior of their population during the recent political campaigns substantiates their irrationality.

Upon our landing, my peer pilot and I left our individual pods behind and immediately walked through the natural region, our original destination because it is located in a low-density residency area, in a country labeled, "United States of America," a sector termed, "Colorado." Native grasses, trees, and small insects in a burgeoning chorus energized the air. I paused on the intruding cement sidewalk when I heard the cries overhead. I looked up to see wild geese aloft, each one with its own distinctive blare, drifting yet coordinated in their flight. The song was spellbinding.

We continued on a path toward the town center. There we saw restaurants, shops, stores, and a delightful mixture of residents of all ages and physical types. We immediately noted the presence of a number of red-haired children, one of the primary reasons we had decided to convene here.

As you know, redheads are special specimens. Humans haven't yet discovered that the type occurs only when conditions in the universe are auspicious. Redheads are more sensitive, intelligent, sensual, intuitive, and talented than the ordinary being. The composition of living entities on our home planet verifies these facts. Most of us are redheads, although we manifest the great variety of physical heights, weights, skin colors and features as do this planet's humanoids. On Earth, the natural occurrence of redheads is small and declining. If humans were considered animals, the gingers would be grouped as "endangered," protected for their rarity.

But not here in Plumbum, my term for our present abode. Is there something in the air, the water, the ground of this community that creates so many redheads? Like radioactive isotopes? Does a mental connection or power somehow reach far into female ovaries to tweak the gene sequence? A mystery to me.

All I know is many things in Plumbum are strange, inexplicable. For instance, a tower on the border of our neighborhood, looming high over the vicinities, is due west of town center. Hundreds of feet tall, a concrete and steel remnant from redevelopment, it stands like a hideous phallic symbol supervising the environs. But as we move south, that tower also moves south inexplicably, across the horizon for no reason. This isn't an optical illusion. Compass points don't behave here like they do elsewhere on Earth. An enigmatic phenomenon. Magic? A supernatural power?

Perhaps this explains the redheads, too. Redheads are a major reason my peer pilot and I came here. Our charge calls for us to discover the cause for their appearance and to increase their manifestation, harness their enigmatic power, to benefit the universe. On Earth, redheads made their appearance at different times and locations. In the Balkans, mysterious tribes of blue-eyed and red-haired warriors were known for their aggressiveness and agility. Half a globe away, Polynesians with auburn hair were thought descendants of high-ranking ancestors and rulers.

We gained much information about redheads from a native male named Reilly, whom we have met several times at one of Plumbum's numerous coffeehouses, writing what he calls "poetry" on his laptop. He has plenty of traumas and miseries to write about, although he ignores those in favor of being positive. "I've been told by various acquaintances that redheads are exceptional, gifted, charming," he says to me. I sit next to him, along with neighbors who indulge themselves in creative endeavors that never will bring financial gain. He tells me these activities are called "arts" and serve to simultaneously explore new ideas and express emotions.

Reilly tells us, unlike the rest of Earth, in Plumbum, redheads comprise a sizable number, and it's growing.

"No one knows why," says Reilly. "Perhaps because Plumbum is like a middle-class asylum, and they feel safe here. Structures are new, homes resemble one another with their carefully tended outdoor furniture and copious flora of dazzling colors, and the residents appear disgustingly healthy, well-dressed, and well-adjusted." Reilly stops to sip his beverage, then stares at me. "I know you said you're a newcomer here, but you fit in perfectly.

More than perfectly." I somehow feel he's tracing the lines of my face.

Can environment affect the appearance of humans even while it modifies intelligence and talents? Seems so. But redhead or not, the entire populace of Plumbum never doubt their position at the apex of Earth's evolutionary ladder. My peer pilot feels any species as self-centered as *homo sapiens* would be challenged not to feel and act superior as this one does. In discussions between us, he says they believe they deserve to rule the world.

That sounds reproving. My apologies. My feelings toward humans are so mixed, from good to ill, it's difficult for me to report objectively.

Nonetheless, many of my opinions reflect my continued interactions with Reilly. Reilly invites us and other natives to a social event called "happy hour." During these times, neighbors imbibe a mood-altering beverage called "beer" that makes individuals feel warm and friendly.

Reilly proclaims himself to be an expert in gingers. "Everyone knows redheads are super-sensitive," he says. "They also have bad tempers, are quick to act, bold, and brash. Red hair is rare, associated with youth, passion, and hot-headedness. Turns out 'carrot tops' also are having more sex than the rest of us, which makes them attractive to others, especially those with strong sex drives or few partners. Mystery surrounds them." Reilly winks in my direction.

Reilly rubs his palm over his bald head. What little hair he has, he shaves religiously, indicating the dedication with which he follows his personal code of honor. Cleanliness, integrity, honesty, thoughtfulness. Plus humor. As devout as a monk. "I used to be red-headed," he says, "when I had hair. Truth be told, redheads are unusual. Both parents must carry the recessive gene, then match up, to win the genetic lottery.

Some people reach out a finger or hand to touch them for good luck." Reilly reaches toward me as he says this, stroking my red hair softly.

You may believe these facts make the probability of this species becoming a productive, positive member of the intergalactic family low indeed. I know that's the opinion of my peer pilot. In our conversations, Reilly conveys to me the fascinating details of a myriad of human belief systems and cultures. For example, he says two universal laws, called *commandments*, govern human interaction. The first: to love their god; the second: to love one another.

Yet they wage war and destroy their fellows with the enthusiasm of a fanatic. Yet they turn away from other humans who are ill, starving, terrified, determined to see nothing inhumane in this attitude. Yet they rob, steal, cheat, and lie to one another as if their lives depend on it. My cardiac organ hemorrhages for them. And yet. . . and yet. . . I believe strongly that *homo sapiens* hold much potential for good.

If they ever discover the true power of the intangible, their own two laws, they will be unstoppable. They feel deeply, understand life completely, far more than any other life form we've studied. The strength of their emotions makes them prime candidates to push the evolution of intelligent life far above the current status. Their world (if rescued from the destructive impact of the negative segment of the species) is so beautiful that I'm willing to wager my very survival on it.

Therefore, you may consider this communication to be my resignation. I will remain here.

I have discovered our species can interbreed.

###

About the Author

Bonnie McCune is a freelance writer in Denver. At age 10 she received a rejection from the *Saturday Evening Post* for a poem, but her interest in writing led to a looong career in public relations for nonprofits while she also freelanced articles and stories.

Her numerous credits and more short stories may be seen at www.BonnieMcCune.com/writing

*****~~~~~*****

The Warrior Rides into Battle, Sword Held High

by Brian Rappatta

The 7:58 that runs the length of Academy Boulevard from north to south is the perfect metaphor for modern-day wage slavery.

It has its regulars. There's Paul. He's twenty-two, assistant manager at the Hot Topic in the north mall. Today he's hunkered in the backmost seat, looking out the window. He's on his way to work. He's still a little pissed that his best friend Ned knocked up that skank three years ago right when the band was on the verge of dropping its first demo tape and left him high and dry and working at Hot Topic. Well, screw Ned, anyway. As soon as Paul's own YouTube solo mixes start racking up the views, Paul will be back on track, and both Ned and Hot Topic could totally kiss his ass.

And then there's Lauren. She doesn't pay much attention to her fellow passengers; she's only riding the bus temporarily. She's saving to buy a car, 'cause really, the bus service in this town is *abysmal*. This creepy-ass bus never even runs quite on time, and there's always some smelly half-drunk dude passed out in the back seat.

159

She's got her eye on a slightly used Honda that she saw on Craigslist. In about another six months or so, she's moving on up, thank you very much. Of course, *nobody* rides the bus because it's convenient, not in this town, but her ex, Brandon, rides the bus lines, too. He rides the east-west line downtown, and once she gets her car she'll never have to risk running into his ass again at the transfer stops. If she sees him again, she's not sure if she'd kill him or fuck him.

And take Jane, the timid pixielike little lesbian who always sits toward the front on her way to her shift at the public library branch, clutching her vinyl tote bag with Ernest Hemingway's likeness on the front. It's obvious she's totally besotten with Heather, the girl who gets on at Oro Blanco and rides just until Barnes, a short stretch by most morning commuters' standards. Paul and Lauren have both noted Jane's googly-eyed sidewise glances at Heather, who always plunks down on the bucket seat directly across the aisle from Jane. Lauren always just rolls her eyes, thinks to herself, *Yeesh, get a room,* and then leans back on her seat and focuses on the Linkin Park in her headphones.

Heather, for her part, isn't entirely oblivious to Jane's attention—she's not blind. If circumstances were different, she might have struck up a conversation with Jane. Jane's really quite cute, in her own *golly-shucks* bashful way, but. . . well, that doesn't seem quite fair, considering that what Jane saw, what she *thought* she saw, isn't quite the real Heather. The auburn wig, after all the chemo, isn't exactly her real hair, and the apocalyptic amount of makeup she needs to make her cheeks not look hopelessly sunken and sallow are a total artifice.

The smile she gave Jane when boarding this morning, though, was entirely genuine, entirely *her.* If circumstances had been different, if Heather had actually been able to bring herself to speak to Jane, she would have thanked Jane for looking at her like. . .

Like people had used to.

. . .

Hi. I'm Jane.

Would that be so hard, really? Would that seem jaunty and friendly like she intended, or would it come off as artificial and artless—or worse, desperate and needy?

There was even a perfectly logical, predestined follow-up if she ever managed to break her paralysis and get past those first few words. *So, I guess you go to work or something every day at this time, too, huh?*

After all, it wasn't as if they hadn't seen each other, smiled politely at each other every day this week already on the 7:58 bus, which always ended up being more like the 8:10 bus as a result of traffic and the shitty bus service in this town.

And *damn,* her smile was so. . . so. . .

Radiant.

Jane didn't quite know why that word popped into her head—was it too cliché?—but hey, if the shoe fit. . .

Radiant. Like a month full of lazy Sundays when you didn't have to work, and all you had to do was lie in bed with a book by your favorite author.

Jane frowned. That analogy was a little strained, but, what the hell-ever. The girl with the soulful green eyes and contemplative gaze that drank in *every* detail of the city outside the bus's window as it flashed past, seemingly the same as every morning but so infinitely infinite in its subtle varieties—

Jane had to catch herself from staring overlong at the girl, lest the girl notice her noticing everything and think she was creepy or something—

The girl *did* have a radiant smile, though. And Jane deluded herself into thinking that it was especially for her, the girl's fellow conspirator on the daily 7:58 AM sojourn that they shared to wherever their destinations were.

Hi. I'm Jane. So, you go to work everyday at this time, huh?

Why was that so hard?

But of course, the words never made it past her hyperactive, caffeine-fueled stream of consciousness.

And today, just like every other day this week, it was too late. The girl always got off at Academy and Barnes, at the same stop. Their eyes met, and she flashed Jane that same radiant smile, and while Jane was still lighting up inside from it, the girl was already down the steps and off the bus.

Jane watched her. It was safe to stare now, because now the girl was part of the landscape outside the bus's window, and that's what everybody on the bus did: they looked out. That was normal. That was to be expected. That's all you could do when you were riding in a metaphor.

The girl with the radiant smile gave a prim little wave and said something to the member of the Cult of the Portly Creator, with his grungy hoodie and Buddha belly, who always trolled this street corner with his ominous signs of doom. Today's read:

THE END IS NIGH

Only 2,379 more words to go.

Jane imagined the girl with the radiant smile even knew his name, because *of course* she would; she noticed things. She noticed people. She noticed.

"Morning, Bob," Jane imagined her saying. "Fine day, isn't it?"

"Radiant," Bob answered.

Jane sighed. *Hi. I'm Jane.*

. . .

And then, today, when the bus stops at Academy and Powers—only two minutes past its scheduled time—Heather doesn't get on, much to Jane's consternation. Her first reaction is, of course, concern, even though she tells herself there's any number of reasons. It's not like she's memorized Heather's schedule. She's not like a stalker or anything. Maybe today was Heather's day off of work, or maybe, with the bus actually coming as close to on time as it had in weeks, Heather had been running late and had missed the bus and would have to wait for the 8:33, which might as well have been a universe away. It's no big, Jane tries to tell herself.

But of course, all this is a lie. And when Heather's normal stop at Academy and Barnes rolls around, Jane surrenders to an unhealthy compulsion and gets off. It's a whole twelve stops too early for her. *What are you gonna do, wait a whole thirty-five minutes and see if she gets off the next bus?* she thinks. *And it's not like there's anywhere to hide. What're you gonna do, just smile and say, "Hi, I'm Jane. I'm stalking you?"*

But she hasn't thought that far ahead. So instead she just stands under the bus stop pretending to look at the posted schedule. It's broad daylight, and a busy street, but she's still a little frightened as Bob from the Cult of the Pot-bellied Creator approaches her.

THE END IS NIGHER.

2,068 more words to go.

his sign reads today.

"This isn't a transfer stop," he tells her. "There's no other line that runs through here."

"I—I'm not looking to transfer," Jane says. "I just. . . I think I just needed some air. Maybe I'll get back on the next bus that comes along."

He looks at her quizzically; she's really not that good of a liar. "Won't that make you late for work?"

"Maybe," she says. "But nobody will notice. I won't get fired."

"I see." A pause. "She's not coming. Not today."

"'She?' She who?"

"You know. *Her.* She always gets off at this stop."

"I'm not sure I know what you—"

"This is my pre-ordained corner," Bob says. "I'm Robert. I think. . . I think you're the one I've been waiting for."

Jane clutches her book bag in front of her. "That's a little creepy-stalkery, Bob."

"Robert. Call me Robert. I hate Bob." He casts a glance up at the sky. "And you're one to talk, Mary Sue. I know this isn't your stop."

"Mary Sue? My name's not Mary Sue."

He blinks. "It isn't?"

"No. I'm Jane. My name's Jane."

His eyes widen. "It *is* you. I've waited for so long."

"Um—"

He flings off his backpack. "You're the chosen one. Only you can save her."

Jane raises an eyebrow. "Save her from what?"

"Stage four renal cancer. She's dying."

"That's. . . that's terrible," Jane says. And she means it. And despite the news coming from a creepy-stalkery dude in a frayed, frumpy hoodie, she oddly has no reason to doubt him.

Bob shrugs. "It's the rules. Where he's concerned," he points up at the empty sky, "it's always crisis and melodrama. There's no such thing as a normal slice-of-life." He unzips his backpack and rummages around in it. "But you're the one. You can save her. Only you."

Jane raises an eyebrow. "Um—"

"Only you can wield the sword of the Powergel." Bob holds something out to her.

"That's not a sword," Jane says. "That's a pen."

He grimaces. "Duh. It's a metaphor. The Powergel is mightier yet than a sword."

"That's a terrible cliché."

He shrugs. "The one I serve is nothing if not lazy."

"And yet you worship him?"

"Worship? Oh, good heavens, no. I'm just his bitch. And he's a totally vengeful, spiteful little fucker."

He taps the side of his nose. "Crisis and melodrama and miserable lives, don't you know?" Bob—Robert—comes closer to her. He extends the Powergel out to her. "Take it. I took it before he could finish her off. Only you can wield it. Only you can use it to defeat him."

Jane takes the proffered pen. She looks at it dubiously. It says PENTECH around the grip. "What does it do?" she asks.

"It breaks down and transcends the barriers."

"What the hell is that supposed to mean?"

"The barriers. You, me, they. . . past, present, future. . . the barriers break down, and all roll into one."

"Huh?"

"Let me show you. What's my favorite color?"

"How should I know?"

"Don't think. Just tell me. What's my favorite color?"

"Purple?"

"Correct. I don't have any other choice, you see." He points up at the sky. "It's *his* favorite color. When's my birthday?"

"I don't know. August twenty-third?"

"Correct."

She thinks about calling him out, calling him some sort of carnival huckster, but somehow she knows he's not lying. "So, it's some kind of telepathy?"

"Oh, no. It's much more than that. It breaks down and transcends the barriers. It makes all times, all points of view, one."

"Yeah, I heard you the first time, but what does that mean?"

He looks nervously at the sky. "I've said all I can. When he discovers I took it from him, he'll. . . " He looks nervously up at the sky. "He'll probably give me a very graphic death."

He scampers away, leaving Jane staring after him, clutching the Powergel.

. . .

Hi. I'm Jane.

So I'm not really sure what I'm supposed to do with this damned thing.

I'm beginning to think Bob's just full of shit.

. . .

Geez, I can't believe I just wrote that. Bob must've really gotten in my head.

I took a break and got up from my desk and held the pen in my palm and started walking through the shelves with no real destination in mind. I know it's dumb, but I thought just maybe the pen would tell me what to do, lead me toward Nirvana, like some kind of divining rod, or some shit like that.

It breaks down the barriers. Dammit, Bob, what the hell is that supposed to mean?

I stopped at a random shelf and pulled the twelfth book from the left out. The book was *Psycho Proctologists and the Flaming Buttholes of Doom.*

Okay, I think it's pretty safe to say the pen wasn't leading me anywhere.

. . .

Hope springs eternal, though. I did some checking in our database—checked out the Pot-Bellied Creator. I used the pen to write down some of his stories on sticky notes. Apparently, we have *nothing* by him on our shelves, nor do any of the other branches in town, 'cause he's apparently a two-bit talentless hack. Barely deserves to be called a writer at all.

Some of his shit's online, though. So I checked it out, and I now I hate myself a little for doing it. It looks like a bunch of schmaltzy trash, like everybody, not just Heather, is dying of cancer. Bob's right. All crisis and melodrama, and *really* bad metaphors. Yeesh.

I'll just read a little. . .

. . .

The Warrior Rides Into Battle

The sheer tedium of the Portly Creator will eventually get to her, just like it did Bob. That, and accidentally forgoing lunch as she reads. But eventually she'll surrender to low blood sugar. She'll drift off, and lay her head down on her desk.

When she wakes up, she'll blink the fuzz of sleep out of her eyes. She'll look out the window opposite her desk. It will be dark outside. Then, she'll check the old analogue clock, the one whose second hand, in the silence of the library, punctuates every *tick tick tock* of her workday: 4:59.

It's Tuesday, which means she'll have to close down the tiny little branch. She'll get up from her desk, and head on her normal circuit through the aisles, checking to see if there are any lingering patrons still perusing the shelves.

As always, the shelves will be clear. But at the back, sitting at the table with the old antique lamp with the green lampshade that Jane keeps threatening to take home some day. . .

Oh, my god. It's him.

The light from the lamp will obscure his face, but she'll know him by his shape. He's pot-bellied, like Bob, and wearing a frumpy old hoodie with frayed edges on the cuffs of the sleeves. He seems to be lost in thought, staring out the nearby window into the darkness that comes so early this time of year. He's tapping a pen—a plain old Bic—onto a notebook open on the table before him, as if in pursuit of an elusive idea. But nothing will come, and he'll stare balefully at the cheapass Bic in his hands, as if resenting it.

Jane will take a step forward, ready to tell him that it's closing time, but the words will die on her lips. She'll realize she's gripping the Powergel in her hand. She won't remember bringing it with her from her desk, but then, she's still going to be a little fuzzy from her too-long nap.

So, instead, she'll take a step forward, hold up the pen, and let the words come to her as they may.

. . .

You're looking for this, aren't you? You seem rather lost without it. Like maybe, just maybe, having the right pen will magically make the words come out right? Give just the right ending to Heather's story?

She has to have life-threatening cancer, doesn't she? She can't just have a little problem like a big zit on her cheek, 'cause who'd want to read about that, right? After all, those are the rules, right?

But that's not much like reality, is it? After all, what's reality but a whole bunch of mostly insignificant little slices of life?

You don't need a special pen to break down the barriers. You don't need a magic MacGuffin in the story. Sometimes all it takes is—

. . .

Today's finally the day. She turns to the girl across the aisle, and today that girl is looking especially radiant even if she does have a giant zit on her left cheek.

She smiles at the girl, and says,

"Hi. I'm Jane."

###

About the Author

Brian Rappatta is a queer expat author currently living in South Korea. His short fiction has appeared in places such as *Analog, Baffling Magazine, Amazing Stories, Writers of the Future, Chilling Ghost Stories* (from Flame Tree Publications), and in multiple podcasts such as *Tales to Terrify, StarShip Sofa, and Curiosities.*

*****~~~~*****

The Best Damned Barbershop in Hell

by Bruce Arthurs

Some demons down here in Hell, they enjoy inflicting torture and pain on human souls. Not me. I mean, hey, yeah, I did it for centuries, but it was just a job for me. Clock in, stab stab stab all day, clock out, and go home to my apartment in Respite.

Oh, yeah, you're new here. You didn't know the City of Dis has a suburb, did you? Respite's a bedroom community, mostly, but it has its share of strip malls, grocery stores, restaurants, and fast food joints. The usual. Decent place for hard-working underdemons to kick back and relax after a hard day in the torture pits.

What? No, there ain't any churches. If you're in Hell, it's way too late to look for help from one of those. Unless you've got an in with one of the Fallen Ones, you're screwed for all eternity. Well, unless you got some kinda special skill that might get you a sponsor.

How's that? Those businesses in Respite I mentioned? They need employees. They're owned by underdemons like me, natch, but none of us get to go into private business until we've served enough time doing the shit jobs in Hell proper.

I had that time in, saw an opportunity, applied for all the permits, and got myself set up to run a little barbershop in one of Respite's strip malls. The permits included the right to pull up to two damned souls from the pits and hire them on as employees.

Pretty sweet, right? I'd had an eye on a woman named Elizabeth for the shop's manicurist since I'd first thought of the barbershop idea. It wasn't like anything she'd done in her living life, but the way Lizzy had axed her parents to death showed a natural talent for trimming things; she just needed a little practice and a little restraint.

I had to pass on my first choice for a barber; I got told by the Fallen One in charge of permits that the inventor whose machine had beheaded hundreds needed at least another century of agonizing punishment. Sanctimonious prick, like all the winged bastards, just because they and their Big Boss were here first. Like underdemons are second-class, just because we're formed from Hell's ruddy clay.

So, I asked an underdemon I knew in Records to pull me up some files, and that's how I found Tony.

Tony hadn't just had experience with sharp blades like Dr. G, he'd been a barber, in a long family line of barbers, and he'd been great at being a barber. He'd had his own shop in Brooklyn, an apartment on the floor above, and a wife, Rebecca, who worked as the shop's manicurist and who was a real looker.

But no kids. Did I mention his wife was a looker? So it wasn't for lack of trying during those first few years of marriage. And then a few more years. And a few more.

But hey, one night Rebecca tells Tony she's finally pregnant. Happy ending, right?

Except Tony hadn't told Rebecca he's seen a doctor privately, and found out he only shot blanks.

Rebecca confesses. She's been sleeping with Roberto, one of Tony's best friends and a regular customer.

The next morning, Roberto comes into the barbershop for his weekly trim and shave. "Morning, Tony," he says, smiling like the lying, treacherous bastard he is. Roberto sees Rebecca's empty workstation. "Where's Rebecca?" he asks.

"She's tied up," Tony answers. He gives Roberto the usual trim and shave, and man, Roberto looks good. Tony is a goddamn artist with clippers and a straight razor, and this is one of his best pieces of work ever.

"You seem quiet this morning, Tony," Roberto says.

Tony wraps a hot towel around Roberto's face. "Oh, I've had a lot on my mind, Roberto," he answers, and draws the straight razor deeply across the bastard's throat.

Then Tony goes upstairs and unties Rebecca. She runs out of the apartment. Tony sits on the bed, razor in his hand, flipping it open and shut. Open. Shut. Open. Shut. He hears Rebecca's scream, then the bang of the shop's door as she rushes out to the street.

Open. Shut. Open. Shut. Open. Shut.

A policeman appears in the bedroom door, gun drawn. "Drop it!" the cop shouts.

Open. Tony lunges forward, and it's "Welcome to Hell" for Tony.

. . .

Tony's one of the sinners in the boiling lake of blood, but after an afternoon with a dinghy and a boathook, I'm able to fish him up from under the other murderers in the lake. Some guys try to float, others let themselves sink. Something to do with the weight of guilt, I think.

"Hey there, Tony. My name's Grimcanker. I hear you're a barber."

171

Tony screams, cowering and whimpering in the end of the dinghy. Not unexpected; when you've spent decades stewing in boiling blood, you'll be an oozing mass of blisters and brisket when you come out. But sinners heal fast when they're not under active torment, and half an hour later I've got the boat ashore, and Tony just looks slightly parboiled and can form coherent words.

I explain the offer to Tony. He looks over his shoulder at the scarlet lake, then back.

"I'm in. Yes! I'M IN!"

So I've got my shop, I've got my employees, I've got a little office in the back where I can kick back and watch my soaps on a portable TV, while Tony and Lizzy do the work. What could go wrong?

For a long time nothing went wrong. I was right about Lizzy having a natural talent for the nail biz, and even cleaning dried blood out of talons and claws didn't faze her. Tony was a little challenged at first, but he learned fast and soon was trimming and styling scales and feathers and quills just as expertly as he did hair.

Word of mouth is the best advertising, and early customers not only came back, they recommended Demon Street Barber & Nails to others. Business grew. I was making decent money and living comfortable. Tony and Lizzy were working long hours, but that's better than unending agony, right? I even had two cots set up in the shop's storage room for when I'd close the shop at night. Then I'd go home, kick back, and spend time with my pet Gila monsters FiFi and Fred.

In retrospect, that was my biggest mistake. Sleep time, leisure time, for the damned? That's just not done. What did Tony and Lizzy do during those hours together alone? Did they talk to each other? Did they get to know each other? Did they come to care for each other?

Did they fall in love?

I saw, sometimes, during business hours, how they'd look at each other with something more than being co-workers in their eyes. How sometimes a hand would brush innocently—yeah, right—against the other's arm. But I ignored it all, didn't let myself think about it, because I had a good thing going, because I didn't want to rock the boat.

I thought nothing of it, either, when Tony asked me questions about Hell, about the Fallen Ones. I figured anyone stuck in one place, forever, who wasn't preoccupied by pain and agony would want to know more about that place.

"So, the Fallen Ones used to be. . . angels?"

"Well, technically they still are, just cast out, cursed, and compelled to run Hell without hope of. . . " I paused, because we never say a particular name here; I pointed a finger upwards instead. ". . . That Guy's Grace or forgiveness."

"I thought G—That Guy—was supposed to be all about forgiveness."

"Sure. When He wants to be. But if He gets pissed, not so much on the forgiveness thing then. Just ask Mister Morningstar." That was a rhetorical suggestion, of course. Underdemons like me rarely get admitted to even the lower floors of that big black tower of glass at the center of Dis, much less the top floor from which Lucifer Morningstar and his fellow Fallen govern Hell. And the idea of one of the damned chatting up Morningstar, like they were at a freakin' cocktail party together or something? Pfft.

"Morningstar's lost all chance at Grace, then?"

"Yeah. Sad, really, considering he's made of Grace."

"He's what?"

"Made of Grace. You humans were first made from the Earth's clay. Underdemons are made from Hell's clay, which I will be the first to admit is not of the best quality. But the angels were created before Earth or Hell or the heavens even existed, so That Guy used some of his own substance, his Grace, to create them."

"Huh."

Tony had more questions about Grace. What was it? What did it do? What did it look like?

"Well, I sure never seen raw Grace myself, Tony. And you ain't likely neither, being, in case you forgot, *IN HELL*. But I heard me some stories, I don't know if any of them is true, but it's supposed to be like. . . light. Like the brightest light there ever was, only it won't burn you or blind you. It makes you. . . pure. Without sin. But that's just a story I heard a few hundred years ago, and you'd think Morningstar would still be sitting cozy if it was true, wouldn't you? Hey, customer just came in. Get to work."

It was after that conversation that Tony upped his haircutting game. He didn't just make every customer look better, he made them look *good*. And considering what some underdemons look like, that was quite an accomplishment.

"Best haircuts in Hell!" Tony would say to each customer when he finished. "Pass the word along."

And the word got passed. Soon, underdemons who'd been going to some of the fancier-schmancier salons in Respite were coming in to my little barbershop instead.

And then, one of the Fallen Ones walks into the shop.

My guts get a chill. Maybe when Hell was a start-up, the Fallen were more hands-on, but nowadays they mostly delegate the actual running of Hell to us underdemons. Once in a while, they'll do an inspection tour or something, rend a few souls just to keep their hand in, but mostly they stick to their black towers in Dis, moping and feeling sorry for themselves. "Oh, woe, I have been cast out of Heaven. Boo hoo, I'm stuck in this lousy place." Give me a break.

Not this guy. He walks into the shop like he owns it—his head nearly scrapes the top of the door frame, and it's a tall door—and looks around with eyes that don't say a thing, but examine everything and everyone in it with a cold appraisal. Like all the Fallen, his wings are furled, tucked tight against his back. I stand stock still, not knowing why the Fallen is here, not knowing what he wants, not knowing what he'll do. His face is still, revealing nothing. My guts are like ice. Like me, Tony and Lizzy are standing motionless, their eyes wide and fearful.

"It has been said. . . " The Fallen One's voice rings out like a bell of the purest metal. ". . . that the best haircuts in Hell are given here."

I find my voice somehow even if it's cracked and wavering. "Y-yes, sir, that's what we say."

Tony speaks up, to my surprise. His voice is stronger than mine. "I've never had a customer complain."

The Fallen One gestures at the barber's chair. "Perhaps a demonstration."

It's not a question. The barber chair can adjust to all the sizes and shapes of underdemons, so it's only the work of a moment to make it accommodate the Fallen's wings and towering size.

The Fallen sits. Tony does the usual for a first-time customer, walking around him, studying structure and features, the customer's current appearance, and how that interacts with the rest of their body. Then he goes to work.

With some of our underdemon customers, Tony's approach is to start with hedge clippers. With the Fallen, it's a fine-toothed comb and his smallest, sharpest scissors. A snip here, a bit of trimming there.

Lizzy rolls her nail table up beside the Fallen. She cleans and files and buffs the big hands' nails, gives them a clear top coat, and buffs again, giving the nails a pearl-like luster.

175

Tony steps back, done. There is less than a handful of trimmings on the floor, but the severe poker face of the Fallen has transformed. The hairline just oh so slightly altered, the eyebrows marginally reshaped, but the overall effect brings a touch of personality to that cold face. Still severe, still serious, but with the possibility of private feeling behind that facade.

Tony spins the chair to let the Fallen see the result in the shop's mirrors. The Fallen looks for what feels like forever. I see one eyebrow rise, then the Fallen nods.

"Impressive," he says.

"Thank you," Tony replies, whisking the barber's drape from around the Fallen's shoulders. "Pass the word around. Best haircuts in Hell."

The Fallen stands and walks to the door, then turns. "I shall do that." He turns again and leaves without another word. The three of us are alone in the shop again.

"Well," I say after a long silent moment. "That was something. Not sure what, but it was something." I see Tony and Lizzy give each other a long look, but I don't know what it means, and I'm too shaken to wonder.

Things go back to normal, and I gotta admit, I'm relieved. Fallen Ones may be the big bosses in Hell, but I'm just fine with their staying in Dis. I'd never seen a Fallen in Respite before, and honestly, I hoped I'd never see one in the shop again.

Right. Three days later, the shop door opens, and another Fallen One enters. This one's even taller than the first, so he has to bend forward as he enters to keep from bonking himself on the door frame. He finishes entering, straightens up. . .

. . . and I see it's not just *a* Fallen One, it's *the* Fallen One. Lucifer Morningstar himself.

I jump to my feet as soon as I recognize him, then stand there bobbing like a loon, uncertain, my mind empty of any guidelines or protocol for something like this. Should I come to attention and salute? Should I bow?

176

Should I go to my knees? Should I prostrate myself on the floor? All those scenarios and more flash through my head and straight back out again.

I look over and see Tony and Lizzy transfixed by the sight of Morningstar. The Fallen Ones were all, so I hear, beautiful before they Fell. We're talking faces like a bun made of handsome topped with double patties of ground handsome and sliced sharp handsome, with handsome lettuce, handsome tomato, handsome pickle, and, why not, some handsome ketchup and handsome mustard. A lot of the Fallen have let their looks go since landing in Hell so long ago. Bags, sallow skin, frown lines, you get the picture.

Not Morningstar, though. He's still got the entire package issued to him in Heaven, plus that roiling internal, eternal anger and outrage that make his eyes flash in a way either terrifying or arousing, if not both. That phrase, "striking good looks"? That's what Tony and Lizzy are experiencing; they're struck dumb.

Seeing them like that breaks me out of my funk. I turn back toward Morningstar and speak. "Uhhhh," I say, getting off to a good start. "What an unexpected pleasure, Mister Morningstar. Welcome to Demon Street Barber and Nails."

My words jolt Tony and Lizzy out of their own fugues. "How can we help you today?" Tony asks.

Two more Fallen enter, a few paces behind Morningstar. One is the Fallen from several days ago. I realize they must be Morningstar's underlings. Had the earlier Fallen One come to scope out the territory before Morningstar's visit? And why was Morningstar here?

And then I look closer at Morningstar, past that oh-so-handsome face and do what I should have done immediately. I check out his hair.

It's. . . not the worst. No hedge clippers required. I'd even call it pretty decent. But the contrast between the meh haircut and that knock-you-back face can't be unseen once it's noticed.

Tony's noticed it too. "Haircut, Mister Morningstar?" He indicates the empty barber chair.

"Yes. I've heard very good things about your work. Yes, I would like a haircut, Tony." He must have done his homework, to know Tony's name. He ignores me. His voice is honey and rose water, polite to a fault but backed by hints of condescension and menace.

Things proceed from there much as they had three days before. Or so I thought. When Lizzy pulls her nail station up, I see how nervous and afraid she is, but I chalk it up to having to work on the Biggest, Baddest, Bad-Ass in Hell. I see some "looks" between Tony and Lizzy, but I figure that's just nerves too. I didn't know they'd been figuring things out. I didn't know they had a plan.

Morningstar is leaned back in the barber chair, eyes closed and, Holy Mother of That Guy, is he *relaxed*? How often does he get a break, even a short one, from having to run Hell? The whole thing about Respite is, we underdemons may be monsters, but we're not actually damned like human souls or the Fallen Ones. We don't *have* to suffer eternally. There are a few scattered exceptions for the others, like the deal with Tony and Lizzy, but I'd never heard of Fallen Ones, especially Morningstar, getting any kind of break from their own damnations.

The two other Fallen are standing near the entrance, looking bored. Lizzy is working on Morningstar's hands, working lotion into the skin. I keep seeing her glancing up at Tony, a nervous look on her face. It worries me, but I stay silent.

"Mister Morningstar," Tony says. "I'll do a razor trim to your neckline. Will that be all right?"

"Mmph. Go ahead."

Tony gets a handful of hot lather from the dispenser and spreads it carefully on Morningstar's neck.

He opens his straight razor and hones it on the strop hanging nearby.

"I'll have to work around your wings, Mister Morningstar. I'll be careful, but it's a bit awkward."

"Go ahead."

I hear the hiss and scrape of Tony's razor on Morningstar's skin. I see what he meant about awkward. The huge wings folded behind Morningstar mean Tony has to twist and bend to reach properly.

"I'll need to reach across your chest for this last bit, sir."

Morningstar just grunts in agreement.

As Tony reaches out, he gives one last look towards Lizzy. Her face is frightened. Whatever they've planned, she wants to change her mind at the last moment. She gives a tiny shake of her head, *No.*

Tony looks at her, then nods his own head, *Yes,* and slashes Morningstar's throat.

A lot happened in the next few seconds.

A bright, bright light erupted from the gash in Morningstar's neck, rushing out like a tight flashlight beam. Morningstar lurched up in the chair, roaring, snatching his hands free from Lizzy and groping upwards.

Lizzy started to rise, shouting "No! Tony—!" But Morningstar's upward lurch brought the beam downwards, made it fall onto Lizzy.

That light, that light of Grace, struck Lizzy and seemed to grow even brighter as it spotlighted her. It was so bright it washed her out in its overwhelming glare, but not before the look of fear on Lizzy's face transformed into one of transcendent Joy.

Tony leapt away from Morningstar, then tried to run forward, to cast himself into the Gracelight along with Lizzy. But the Fallen Ones by the entrance had sprung into action, bounding across the shop floor and grabbing Tony by his arms, yanking him back.

Morningstar clutched at his throat. The beams split into smaller rays as his fingers blocked them. He growled, adjusted his grip, squeezed the cut edges of his throat together. The beams shrank, dwindled, then vanished as the edges healed shut within seconds.

Lizzy was. . . gone.

I saw all this, because as soon as that Gracelight had burst out, I'd scrambled away in panic, climbing the wall and ending up hanging from the ceiling in the farthest corner of the shop. I had no idea what exposure to Grace would do to an underdemon, but I didn't want to find out. I dropped back down and tried to hide behind a chair as Morningstar slowly straightened and turned towards Tony.

I'll say this for Tony: He put on a brave front, standing straight and facing Morningstar with only a moderate amount of trembling and quaking.

Wrath lightninged across Morningstar's features as he glared at Tony. And then he made an odd, hiccup-like kind of sound. And another. Then a bunch, and I realized Morningstar was chuckling. The chuckling grew louder, became booming laughter that filled the shop with sound.

Morningstar wiped at his eyes, gasping. "Oh. Oh my. That was a good one. I did not see that one coming at all."

In my hiding spot, I started thinking maybe Tony would get through this after all.

But then the laughter vanished from Morningstar's face, and that face became terrible to behold.

"You reminded me of what I used to be," he said to Tony. "I will hurt you for that." And then he unfurled his wings.

HE. UNFURLED. HIS. WINGS.

What I remember seeing, what I think I remember, before seizure and blackness overtook me, were no feathers, no fur, no covering of any kind on the underside of those wings. Bare, pale skin, but not empty skin, for

180

there were words written there. Words of expulsion, words of condemnation, words that denied all hope or forgiveness. Words shaped in G— in That Guy's own handwriting.

Words written in scars.

Morningstar loomed towards Tony, and wrapped his wings around him, and that was when I passed out, twitching and trying to choke on my own tongues.

When I regained consciousness, the shop was empty. No Tony, no Morningstar, no Fallen Ones. No one, except poor miserable Grimcanker. the unluckiest underdemon in Respite, if not in all Hell.

So, you won't be surprised to learn that my application to bring in new souls to work in the shop got turned down. I had a shop, but no way to run it. I had to close it down, and come back to work here. Maybe after another five or six hundred years the black mark on my record will have faded enough to try being a shopkeeper again. Maybe a sandwich shop next time.

Whoa, look at the time! Just one more thing I wanted to mention.

After a while, curiosity got the better of me, and I asked my friend in the Records Office to find out just what happened to Tony. I thought maybe there was a human-skin rug in Morningstar's office, one that cried out in pain whenever it was walked across.

And what my friend found was. . . nothing. Nothing at all. It was as if Tony were completely erased from Hell's files. As if he'd never existed at all. And when my friend tried to dig a little deeper, he got told to drop his inquiries or face consequences. Serious consequences.

Here's what I'd like to think, and I'll admit maybe this is just wishful thinking, but I wonder: Could Tony have earned his own salvation by arranging it for Lizzy? After Morningstar snatched Tony from the barbershop, could That Guy have snatched Tony's soul away from Morningstar in turn? Did Tony earn himself a place in

Heaven? And if he did, does that mean other damned souls could be forgiven and saved as well?

What? No, hey, don't thank me. I'm just a blabbermouth underdemon who likes to yap with humans sometimes. I didn't *mean* to give you any hope. I could get in a lot of trouble if you say that kind of thing. Don't tell anyone where you heard that last part, okay?

Anyway, gotta toss you back in the boiling blood now. Sorry. Nothing personal; it's just my job for a few more centuries. But hey, if you run into any good sandwich makers down there, let me know, okay?

About the Author

Bruce Arthurs has written occasional stories since 1975, with more than 20 short stories in various magazines and anthologies over the years. A 1990s foray into screenwriting led to writing an episode of STAR TREK: THE NEXT GENERATION ("Clues", 4th Season, 1991). He edited the anthologies *Copper Star* and *Olympus*. After a long hiatus, he began writing fiction again in 2012 while recovering from a badly broken arm. Notable stories published since then include "In the Days of Mister Cuddles" in Third Flatiron's *Strange Beasties* anthology, "Beks and the Second Note" in *Alfred Hitchcock Mystery Magazine*. He was a Best Short Story nominee for the 2017 Derringer awards, and most recently published "In the Armpit" (*Cosmic Horror Monthly*).

He's been a US Army company clerk, a legal secretary, had a 30-year career with the USPS, and as a security officer before retiring in March 2020. (Good timing to start spending every day at home!) He lives in Arizona with his wife Hilde, several housemates, and a small mob of cats.

*****~~~~*****

The Girl Who Built Worlds

by Alicia Cay

I am going to see the sun rise. I'm going to watch it crest over the surface of that planet hovering before me, the flares of its light so intense it will fill every cell of every fiber of my being.

The sun is set to rise in approximately thirteen minutes.

I glance at my screen display. The alarms, having been silenced, blink back at me in crimson warning.

I've got eleven minutes of life-support left.

. . .

I have always been different, not like other girls. I blame Grandpa Joe for this. He was a sergeant on the very first Builder Crew, back when the Outer was more like the Wild West and they rode rocket ships out past the boundaries of science and good sense.

"There was a time, Nina," Grandpa told me when I was eight, "when our world forgot about Pluto as a planet at all. Little did we know the secrets she kept." He laughed his gravel-lined laugh, and I snuggled further into the crook of his arm, breathing in the apple-smoke scent of his favorite cigars. The only bad habit he ever admitted to.

Perhaps my life would have been easier but for Grandpa Joe. He filled my head with stories of the stars, and in doing, stole away the future Mum was grooming me so hard to have. I don't believe she ever forgave him for that. She made sure I paid her price for it, too.

I have always been smart, the smartest girl. The daddy-long-legs of it is, that in order to do the type of work I had set my heart on doing, the type of work Grandpa Joe had done, I had to be more than smart. "You've got be tougher 'n titanium siding too," Grandpa would say. "Show 'em what you're really made of."

I didn't know then what I was really made of.

I'm still not sure.

Maybe I did have to work harder to make it. That was okay. I wanted it badly enough to put the effort in. It took me a decade of physical and mental training before I qualified to be on a World-Building Crew. On my thirtieth birthday, Mum weeping on the vid-phone, I signed up. My rebellions have always been quiet.

So here I am.

I've done it.

Everything I set my mind to.

Except, I'm not supposed to die out here! After I've left my mark on this existence, I'm headed to the luxury planet, Serena12, where I will live out the rest of my life in relaxation. See? I've already got the entire plan worked out. It can't end like this!

I close my eyes, as if it will block out this mirage future shimmering within me, and I see Elmore, my crew-twin. We were assigned to one another on my first day, and unlike most crew-twin couples, we've beaten the odds and worked together for over six years.

He has no idea I'm in love with him.

We've shared enough of ourselves for me to know that he is supposed to be my *one*.

Now instead, he'll retire to Serena12 and get married—only not to me.

A flare of light glances off the planet spinning there, below my heels, it burns its way beneath my eyelids, imprinting the vision of Elmore and some other woman. His dark eyes will drink her in, as she throws back her sunshine hair and strokes his long eyelashes with her perfect slender fingers. I hate her.

I see it all. They're at home together, living in *my* house, with red-brick walls and a hummingbird garden out back where the children—*our* children—play, except Elmore is calling them by different names.

This can't be happening.

This isn't right.

I'm destined to leave my mark on this existence as a pioneer, a hero! Aren't I?

I've done things that matter. Baby suns are growing to maturity at the centers of freshly spun planetary systems; they feed on its light and warmth because of what I've done—me!

Heroes don't end like this.

I can't die like this.

Alone.

I blame Grandpa Joe. He put these stars in my eyes—damn him, anyway.

. . .

The planet dancing before me in section 0103 of the Outer was seeded here by another Builder Crew years before my arrival. Hand-crafted and designed by scientists on Earth, it's more beautiful than anything Grandpa Joe was ever able to describe.

It's a bit like Earth (the earlier ones often are), with swirling hues of greens and blues, yet its differences are striking. One of the lab-geeks has added colors of surprise. Some mineral composition in the ground casts shades of purple along the contours of the planet's curves, while lavender streaks fall along its valleys, and plum shadows trace the edges of its rocky peaks.

I'm gagging.

The clot of disaster in my throat is growing larger. I suck in, then choke on a lungful of air. My O2 meter is spinning at the use of precious oxygen.

Elmore's voice slips into my mind. "Check yourself, newbie. Before you go and wreck yourself."

At his phantom words, I slow my breathing, and force myself into some weak semblance of calm.

I will never see him again.

Salty tears slip down my face, escaping like prisoners from behind eyelid gates. My lips twist into a savage mimicry of a scream, silent and breathless, so as not to waste any more air. My arms jerk reflexively, I want to wipe the tears away, but coated as they are in the deadly red cloud of astro-microorganisms clinging to my suit, I can hardly bend them anymore.

This is all Elmore's fault! He left me out here.

I work my arms against their crimson-colored bindings. My chest is tight, pulling on the muscles in my upper back. The cloud of Red Tide is still gathering on my suit, weighing down my arms and legs. All movement feels impossible. I am being slowly frozen, cast in a plaster of scarlet disaster.

I cry.

I struggle harder.

I scream.

How far did the ship go to clear the Red Tide from its engines? Too far, I'm sure. There is no way for Elmore to make it back to me in time. They had to go, had to save themselves.

Once more it's Elmore's voice that comes, until I am calm again. When I first met Elmore, I stuck out my hand in greeting.

"I don't like newbies," Elmore said, keeping his hands busy and not touching mine.

"We don't like you either," I responded, my voice deadpan. Didn't he know what I had accomplished to get here?

Elmore's head tilted back, and a murder-of-crows clatter emerged from his mouth. He never did laugh quietly. "We might just be in trouble then."

He went on to tell me how his last crew-twin suddenly up and died in a tragic gravitational accident. The details were gory, but Elmore didn't spare them. "He was a newbie too," he said. "I'd just gotten him broken in. So, do me a favor and don't get killed." The light in his dewy eyes dimmed. "I didn't take his death well." He looked at me, his eyes tracing lines from my toes to my hairline. "Yours might just do me in."

That was it: the moment of my undoing.

I worked for ten years, hell-bent-for-leather, to build up my walls, get tough, and this loud-mouthed man-child had found the chink in my fortress in sixty seconds.

The trouble was further exasperated by his chocolate milk eyes, his penchant for cheap, apple-wood cigars, and a New England sense of humor so dry it made the Sahara look like a damn rainforest. Everything was an adventure to him. My grandpa would have adored him.

My heart aches. My fists clench, crunching around handfuls of Red Tide. "Elmore," I yell into my mic. Of course there's no answer, I have drifted too far away by now.

And he let me go.

. . .

The ruby-tinted darkness around me yields no mercy. It hangs on me, pitiless. I cry until there is nothing left, not anger, not even the comfort of static in my helmet's speakers.

Tendrils of sadness pull tight, like shoelaces in my chest. I am no longer in control. Have I ever been? I live my life in appreciation of science, and I have dreamed of soaring beyond the stars of the Outer since Grandpa Joe taught me to walk. I never bothered to worry over who put these stars here. But now? Now I pray.

Grandpa Joe is gone, Elmore is gone, even Mum is gone. Who is left to listen? No one, save some far-off hope that something larger in spirit than I might hear me.

Hadn't I worked hard enough? I can work harder!

Hadn't I given up enough? I celebrate no holidays, take no vacations. I can do more!

I will serve in solitude. I'll go to one of the Devotion Planets and become a Monk. I will live on whatever mountaintop you want. Please!

Once, when I was nine years old, my Mum, worrying at the influence of Grandpa on me and the lack of God (and dresses) in my life, dragged me to church with her; we stood, we sat, we prayed in mournful sounds. It was awful.

I pouted. I crossed my arms and kicked at the back of the pew in front of me. When we got home, Mum went straight to her 'special' cabinet. She didn't even stop to grab a glass.

That night, her eyes red and her lips chapped, she'd taken Dad's belt to my back and legs, swearing she would beat the devil out of me until I acted like a proper lady.

The following night, when Grandpa saw the trouble I had sitting down to family dinner, he made up an excuse to keep me at his house for a week. Grandma Mae put cold cloths on my welts, and Grandpa let me cry as he held me close. He told me his stories and promised me there was something bigger than all of us. "A Maker, an Author of Existence," he said, "lives in the Outer, somewhere among the glittering stars. I promise you, my darling."

I had not given it another thought. Until now. I have been looking for proof of it all along, haven't I?

. . .

The hiss of my failing respirator folds in over my shallow breaths, the sound a constant reminder of what is coming. I close my eyes against the inevitable, and the slow revolution of the purple planet below.

I need the planet to spin faster, I pray for it to spin faster. I beg.

I need it to move, to bring into view that clear radiant burst of light rushing to rise over the ledge of a planet that we, the Builder-Crews of Earth, placed here.

Only two inevitabilities remain now: The sun *will* rise over the far edge of this planet, and I *am* going to die.

Tears crawl down my face; they tickle the sensitive nerve endings along my cheeks. The cruel things bring with them memories of the last time death looked in my direction.

His name was Bow, like the boy's name, only when I named him, I didn't know how to spell it that way. A classic mutt, Bow was sandy-haired, short-legged, and he fit perfectly into the hollow of my tummy as I cuddled around him in bed each night. He was my best friend.

It was a Tuesday morning. I ran from the house to catch the school bus and found Bow in the street.

He did not move.

He could not move.

He was gone.

My howls brought Mum to the front door, a glass already in her hand (not even nine o'clock in the morning).

"Warned you about leaving that side gate open, didn't I?" she said. The ice in her glass tinkled as she shook it in the direction of the fence.

I sat on my knees in the street next to Bow, rocking back and forth as the agony grew in strength and tenor, until Mum had to call Grandpa Joe to come get me.

He took the old quilt from his backseat and wrapped Bow in it. Then he drove me around until I pointed to the place. A small patch of old bent Pine trees close to Grandpa's backyard.

Not even Grandpa Joe's death years later hurt that bad. Maybe because Bow had been my first, or maybe

191

because every morning I let Bow out first thing to use the yard, so I always made sure the gate was locked tight. Mum had come in through it last night after church.

She did it on purpose.

I have always held out secret hope that one day, when I retired, I would find a new Bow. I inhale, and a sharp, hot thing sears into my chest like a brand. That day will not come.

. . .

I should have no expectation of surviving my time working in the Outer, but knowing it's coming, really happening, watching its painfully slow approach as my life-support clock counts down, I realize no amount of training or imagination could have prepared me for this.

What I wouldn't give for a single second more.

I would tell Elmore how I feel about him. I would write down all my stories and dedicate them to Grandpa Joe. I would forgive Mum.

I know, I know. These thoughts are a coward's reaction, my selfish desire to stave off the acidic sensation currently gnawing on my insides.

My eyelids droop. My breathing is shallow. The sweat on my palms is cool. Clammy.

The terror will finish me off if I let it.

I am terrified.

I kick my legs. I need to run, need something tangible to fight against. My adrenaline monitor beeps. I want to claw out the eyes of Death. Don't you know, Death? That you should tremble to take me—ME!

I look at my screen display. I stop moving. The air circulating around me will last another sixty seconds. The sun will be fully risen two minutes after that.

Once my O2 is depleted, I will hold my breath for as long as possible. After that I will begin to suffocate to death.

The sun climbs higher, like a slow hiker, over the purple cliffs of this not-Earth planet, and suddenly,

192

because I know this is the last thing I will ever see, I miss home.

Oh, I get it now.

I understand.

I am here to see it all.

. . .

My final resting place is to be among the same stars that Grandpa Joe put in my eyes. I am to be but a speck of debris in the Universe. So small a thing in so big a place.

That can't be right.

The O2 is gone. Fire lives in my chest. There is a gentle tug around my middle, like the arms of a lover sliding about my waist, and I know the sensation for what it must be. I am slipping from my body.

It's very cold in the Outer.

It's very cold in here.

The sunlight stretches its arms over the surface of the planet, and like shining rays of hope, they grow. It's more than a vision, I can hear it. Swelling to a crescendo, it sings like a chorus of the Divine.

The glare of light, so bright now, reveals itself in slow-motion. It is fire-lit beauty and blinds me in a wash of heat so intense that, for a moment, I feel alive again.

The tug around the middle of my body is still there. It's as though someone has unzipped my suit, my skin, and I'm stepping out of it, drifting backward. I have been waiting to exhale, and now, unable to hold the last vestiges of breath within anymore, my lips sputter outward.

Something is there, on the edge of my senses. Constant static in my helmet. It breaks up and reforms in rhythmic bursts of sound. So much like words. I can't understand them! Only my crew would have been close enough to transmit to me anyway, but Elmore left me. Didn't he?

The light is so bright. It beckons. Then blackness spreads as if someone has thrown a blanket over me, wrapped me in the quilt from Grandpa Joe's backseat.

No matter.

I did it.

I watched the sunrise.

Less static. Now a voice. The voice of the Absolute Answer. Though it sounds so much like Elmore I want to throw my head back and bellow out a laugh that begins in the soles of my feet.

No air left.

I drift backward, pulled away from the purple planet and the risen sun.

The voice comes again, crystal clear this time. "We've got you, Nina. I've got you."

It sounds so much like Elmore.

About the Author

Alicia Cay is a writer of Speculative and Mystery stories. Her short fiction has appeared in several anthologies, including *Hold Your Fire* from WordFire Press, and *The Wild Hunt* from Air and Nothingness Press. She suffers from wanderlust, collects quotes, and lives beneath the shadows of the Rocky Mountains with a corgi, a kitty, and a lot of fur. Find her at aliciacay.com

*****~~~~~*****

One Last Thing
by Danielle Mullen

"We have time for one more question," said the moderator, a young woman in a blue sheath dress patterned with little Captain America shields. Avery thought they were polka dots when she first saw them. It felt like a metaphor for the whole weekend: seeing something and thinking she knew what it was, only to find out it was something entirely different.

"Yes, in the pink." Another volunteer handed off a microphone to a girl who didn't appear to be old enough to drive. Her 1950s style get up was probably a costume, but Avery had no idea who she was supposed to be.

"I was wondering (giggle) if Louis Reilly's looks were (giggle) inspired by someone you really knew?" Giggle.

She wanted to say that even if Louis Reilly's looks were based on a specific man, he would probably be dead by now. She knew her impulse was related to being hungry and tired, but that didn't make it any less tempting. Why did they schedule her for the last panel of the day?

Shouldn't an elderly woman be given an earlier slot? It was already well past her usual dinner time.

"Not one specific person, but there were things about him I took from different people in my life."

"Who?" asked the moderator. Avery wanted to remind her that she already answered the last question, but instead she paused and stared off into the crowd, like she was trying to remember something.

"I gave him my husband's eyes," she said finally, shrugging.

As if on cue, the whole audience made an "Aw" noise. The moderator reminded the audience that Ms. Moran would be signing books at her table tomorrow and available for photo ops in the afternoon. A young man, whose name she forgot hours ago, escorted her off the stage. He wore a t-shirt with a spaceship on it. She thought the spaceship might be from Star Wars or Star Trek, but she'd rather have a sandwich than a conversation right now.

"Please wait here a minute, I need to check on the car," the young man instructed, gesturing towards an open doorway. Inside the room were a few cushy chairs and an empty water cooler with a stack of plastic cups next to it. She took a seat and wished for a granola bar. Her lunch with several of the other guests earlier that day was hours ago. Actors and comic book artists, mainly. All of them were very young, polite, and considerate. She didn't understand why her friends complained so much about the younger generation. In her limited experience, they tended to be much kinder than she ever was at their age. She couldn't imagine her twenty-five-year-old self patiently attempting to find common ground with an elderly woman who didn't even work in the same industry.

She felt like she'd been talking all day. At lunch, at her table, and then the panel. Her usual days at home were never so busy. It was crossword puzzles in the morning and a nap in the afternoon. Sometimes she watched an old movie in the evening. She went out with friends and family on occasion but never for more than a few hours. Her body was no longer used to so much activity.

Perhaps her son, Killian, was right when he told her not to come. But she was curious when she received a phone call from a friendly young woman. Her granddaughter loved such things and was forever sending pictures of amazing costumes she'd made herself. Dr. Myers advised her to keep active and try new things at her last checkup. But maybe this thing was a little too new. Perhaps she should have taken up something more old-ladylike. She could have joined a book club or tried bingo. Except neither of those things interested her in the slightest.

Avery got the strange feeling she wasn't alone and looked up from her fruitless search of her bag for something to eat. Standing at the door was Louis Reilly. Well, not actually him but one of the people dressed like him. A "cosplayer," as they called themselves. She didn't remember this young man from the signing earlier, though there must have been at least forty of them. All of various genders, ages, and ethnic backgrounds. It surprised Avery, since she'd never thought of Louis Reilly as particularly likeable. Emotionally damaged, rude, a liar, and hopelessly romantic to his own detriment. There wasn't much virtue to him beyond his skill at solving mysteries.

Unlike most of the others, this cosplayer actually bore a very strong physical resemblance to Louis Reilly. Not the actor who played him in the 1960s film, but the picture in her head. The picture she'd carried for almost sixty years now. He was alike even down to the ink stains on his cuffs and the startling blue of his eyes. Avery wondered if he was wearing special contacts to get his eyes that shade.

"Are you here to escort me to the car?" she asked.

"No, I was looking for something and got lost," he said. It was a lie. She couldn't explain how she knew.

Nothing in his outward expression betrayed the falsehood, but he was definitely lying.

"What, exactly, were you looking for?"

"You're Avery Moran." It was not a question.

"I'm signing autographs at my table tomorrow. And there will be pictures, too." She didn't understand why anyone would want a photo with some old lady they didn't even know. She could, sort of, see why they'd want one with an actor. People usually knew who actors were and would be impressed seeing their friend with someone famous. But would anyone be impressed by a picture with her?

"I don't want. . . that is, I am not looking for an autograph."

"Sure." Not a lie. *Interesting.* Avery thought. She waited, knowing if she created enough silence, most people would say almost anything to fill it up. Killian fell for it all the time when he was little. Even now there were times when all she had to do was shut her mouth and wait for the truth to come out.

But the cosplayer didn't seem bothered by the silence. He walked over to the water cooler and tried to fill a cup, but only a weak dribble came out. He set the cup down on the table, pulled out a candy bar from his jacket pocket, and tore open the wrapper.

"Want some?" he asked.

"Maybe your eyesight isn't so good, because I'm clearly old enough to know not to take candy from strangers."

"Except I'm not a stranger."

Not a lie either. She wondered if he might be one of those fans who had trouble telling reality from fantasy.

"Okay." Avery said, holding out her hand. She was starving, and if he was going to kill her, "Poisoned by Obsessed Fan Dressed as Writer's own Character" did make for a pretty interesting headline. Or, more to the point: "PI Louis Reilly Murders his Creator."

He broke the bar in half and handed her the slightly larger piece. She thought that was gentlemanly of him.

Avery bit into the candy. She did not recall any sweet ever tasting this good. Chocolate mousse and creme brulee had nothing on the confection of chocolate, caramel, and peanuts she was eating right now.

"Thank you," she said after swallowing a couple of bites. She felt better. She now wished she hadn't had that nasty thought about the girl in pink earlier. After all, even if he didn't exist, Louis Reilly was still a pretty good looking guy. Avery remembered having a very big crush on Fitzwilliam Darcy many years ago. Fictional people did have advantages over real ones. Their behavior was almost always predictable and reliable. And when it wasn't? Well that was never her fault.

"Do you think about death a lot?"

The question shocked Avery for a moment. It was as if he'd heard her earlier thoughts. On the other hand he probably could tell just by looking at her that death was something she contemplated often.

"Well, it's the last big thing I have to look forward to, isn't it?" she joked, but he didn't laugh.

"Would you like some water?"

"Yes, please."

He disappeared and returned quickly holding two water bottles damp with condensation. He opened one before handing it off. It seemed presumptuous, but the fact was she couldn't quite open the damned things anymore. Her hands weren't what they used to be. They weren't the only parts of her that didn't work so well now.

"What brings you here?" she asked, after taking several sips. "To the convention," she added in case he thought she was questioning why he was wandering around in an area where he wasn't allowed.

"Oh, I came with one of the guests."

"Which one?"

"You should drink up. People who don't live in the desert don't realize the importance of hydration until it's too late."

Avery took another sip of water as she reconsidered her friends' thoughts on young people. She knew he was right, but did he have to be so blunt about it?

"Are you enjoying the con?"

"It is. . . interesting. I wrote the last Louis Reilly book almost fifty years ago, so I rarely think about him these days. The idea that people not only read them but reread them, discuss them, and dress up like Reilly—" Avery nodded towards the young man who now had a smug smile on his face. She didn't think there was anything to be smug about, since the most convincing part of his costume was his looks, and he certainly couldn't take credit for those. "How could such a small part of my life become such a big part of so many others'? I met a little girl named 'Reilly.' One man told me the books got him through his father's death. There was even a woman who met her wife because she saw her reading a copy of *The Thing with Feathers* on the bus, and they struck up a conversation. It's odd to think that something I wrote could alter the course of people's lives."

"You're a good writer."

"Thank you, but good writing is one thing. This is something different. It's as if Reilly is a person in their lives. An important one. How can people feel that deep a connection with such an arrogant and broken man?"

"Maybe because he is broken."

"Sure." Avery repressed the urge to roll her eyes.

"I mean, if he was smart and kind and polite and well adjusted—we'd hate him, wouldn't we? He's not perfect, and he knows that, but he still gives the best of himself to the world. He clearly cares very deeply for people, even if he isn't always all that good at expressing those feelings. Seeing someone like that do so much good gives broken people hope."

"So everyone here is broken?"

"Maybe not as badly as Reilly. But we all have our cracks and rough edges. Sometimes we need to be reminded that they don't have to stand in the way of bringing something good into the world."

"He's not real."

"So there was never a fictional character that mattered to you? Some who inspired you? Gave you hope?"

"I suppose there were one or two. Jo March. Elizabeth Bennett. Jane Eyre. Women who didn't quite fit in and spoke their mind."

"I wonder why that is." His tone was teasing. She couldn't recall the last time a young man teased her. Or even really looked at her. It wasn't something she ever thought she'd miss.

"I didn't even want to write, you know? I didn't mind working to put my husband through medical school, but I thought I'd get a nice job in an office. Or maybe a bank. Then I found out I was going to have a baby."

"And that was a problem?"

"For potential employers in the late 1950s it certainly was. No one was going to hire a pregnant woman, so I had to figure out something else. I went to college with someone who worked in a publishing house, so I asked his advice and he suggested I try romance novels. I read a few and tried to write one, but I never got past the first chapter. I've always been fond of mysteries, so I tried a detective novel instead."

"*A Charmed Web She Weaves.*"

"They loved it. They just had one big problem with the detective."

"They didn't like me?" he joked.

"Oh, they liked you. They didn't like your name: Finola Reilly."

He looked surprised. Avery was a little surprised herself. She'd never told anyone that before. Perhaps all those questions at the panel loosened up something inside her.

"I was a woman?"

"Yes. They said no one would buy a hard-boiled female detective. So I changed the name and nothing else."

"Funny how that worked out. Do you ever wish you'd fought them on that point and she was still Finola?"

"I don't know—you go changing one thing, and you change everything. If I'd never gotten pregnant, I'd probably never have started writing. If Reilly was a woman, maybe people wouldn't feel the same about her as they do him."

"For want of a nail. . ."

"Something like that." Avery shrugged. "No point in wondering anyway, the past can't be changed."

"But the future is full of possibility."

"Not much future left in my case," she joked. Again, he didn't laugh. This close to him she could tell he wasn't wearing contacts. But she noticed that while his eyes were the same color as James's they weren't alike in every way. This young man's eyes seemed older, sadder. "I hope your life is less lonely than Reilly's," Avery added, only realizing how rude the remark was after it left her mouth.

"You can write new stories, you know? There's still time. Finally give Reilly the happiness that always eluded him. Or her."

"Would Reilly even know what to do with a happy ending?"

He chuckled at that.

"I suppose you're right. He'd probably end up ruining it the next day. But endings don't really need to be happy to be good."

"I'm sure there's other stories that need to be told more than his. I think Reilly's time is already long past."

"And yours?"

"Nothing left to say."

"I really don't believe that."

"You've certainly got Reilly's optimism."

"Thanks."

Avery got the feeling he was thanking her for something else, but she wasn't certain what.

"I have to go, here—" He opened the other water bottle and passed it to her. She realized she'd finished the first one already. "Take this one too."

She took the bottle and sipped, watching him leave. In the doorway he turned back and smiled at her for a moment. She found herself reflexively smiling back.

"Goodbye, Louis." She expected to feel silly calling someone by a fictional character's name, but she didn't.

"See you around, Avery."

She stared at the empty doorway for a moment, trying to talk herself out of the foolish thought that passed through her mind. She could laugh at herself: just another old woman grown fanciful in her dotage. She needed to stop making fun of Peg for talking to her plants.

After drinking more water, Avery decided to blame her silliness on the dehydration and not her age. She pulled out the convention schedule. There was a banquet tonight, but she'd begged off, instead planning on a quiet night catered by room service. She didn't want to go this morning, but now she found she didn't want to be alone. It was a rare feeling.

The young man in the spaceship t-shirt had returned. He looked a little sheepish and was holding a water bottle out for her.

"Sorry that took so long. They'd already sent the cars out by the time I got there, and so I had to wait for one to get back. Don't worry, I made sure the driver won't leave without you."

"Thanks and thanks but I've already got a water." She held up the partial bottle and waved off his offered one.

"That's good. It's easy to get dehydrated in the desert."

"So I've heard."

"Back to the hotel?"

"Actually, I was wondering, is it too late to go to the banquet?"

"Not at all." The young man offered Avery a hand up and she kept holding onto his arm like it was senior prom and he was her escort. He didn't seem to mind.

"Star Wars or Star Trek?" she asked, nodding toward the young man's shirt.

###

About the Author

Danielle Mullen's work has appeared in print and online, most recently in the *Vex Me No More* anthology. She lives and writes in Southern New Mexico.

*****~~~~~*****

Zeno's Paradise

by E. J. Delaney

"The swings, *Dj'doose*."

She's said her goodbyes, and we've an hour's grace. She takes my hand and we walk slowly down to the park. She's patient, my granddaughter, matching steps with me and soaking up the early morning warmth. I think I understand. She wants something of our history together; something simple and real.

It's been months since we came here and not the hospital; almost a year.

"Do you want a push, *V'noochka*?"

"*Nye, Dj'doose*."

Iulija settles onto the rubber sling. With gum trees at her back and bark at her toes, she takes hold of the chains and kicks out against the air. Her feet are bare, her jeans frayed at the ankles. She wears the top I gave her with the manga-style Ukrainian soldier girl; brave and beautiful, too young to die.

She gains height. Soon she's swinging back and forth, the pendulum of some vast unseen clock. She is calm; serene. Only her hair is in turmoil.

Iulija has always had nice hair. (I did, too, as a young man; now I've nothing but grey halo stubble where my hat sits.) When she pulls away, her chestnut curls fall forward, and she disappears behind them. She hides deep within herself, owlish in the shadows. When gravity takes her, she emerges again with locks streaming, face bare to the sunshine.

We find peace in this last hour—me watching, Iulija swooping then soaring from end to end of the moment. Brush strokes ink the memory.

Here, now, we have all the time in the world.

. . .

"Are you sure, Dj'doose?"

She's talking about me, not her. The clinic doors close behind us, and she tries again to understand the choice I've made. Me, with my MRI scans as clear as Synevyr Lake.

"*Tak*." I squeeze her hand. "Your mama is grown, V'noochka, and for your *baboos'r* three times now we have celebrated Provody. Yet, love still brings up the sun. You cannot deny Dj'doo his one last pleasure in life!"

"But it might not work."

I nod. *Now* she is talking about her.

"True. But if you can be brave, V'noochka, then so can I."

We meet our companions in the waiting room: Dale, who was once a personal trainer; and Jinnie the flame-haired architect. There are others, too, all around the world; but we four have been here from the start.

"We'll run so fast," Jinnie murmurs. Her eyes glaze towards the future. "Just like Doctor Z says. Just like Achilles. And when the tortoise plods on and leaves us behind, we'll chase those first few steps. We'll chase him forever."

We pause to consider this. A word tears free from Dale's withered chest:

"Poetry."

It sounds bitter at first, and heralds an anguish of coughs; but as he rides these out, his grimace turns first rueful then jocose.

"And while you're busy running, I hope you'll find time to draw me up a nice little tortoise-shell bungalow."

"A flying palace for me," Iulija puts in.

Jinnie smiles. "Yes, all right. And what about you, Anatoly?"

"I think perhaps one of these bunkers," I say, nodding slowly. "Just big concrete box, you know?" They look at me, and once I'm sure they think I'm serious, I add: "With flat roof on top for flying palace to land, isn't it?"

Soon Dr Zátopková is with us, and we move to the theatre. We are settled into pairs of adjoining beds: Dale and Jinnie; Iulija and me. Technicians connect us to the quantum computer; nurses to the EKG machines.

"You must send word to me," Dr Zátopková reminds us. "However long it takes you to 'scape the technology; remember, I'll be holding my breath. I want to know everything!"

Four anaesthetists enter the room, masked and gloved for the end of days. Iulija turns her head.

"I'm scared, Dj'doose."

"I know, V'nooch. *Serden'ko.*" We clasp hands. Her fingers are soft against the roughness of my skin. "I'm here. This is only the beginning."

"That's right," Dr Zátopková gushes. She seems at the last more maiden aunt than laureate in waiting. "You have the whole of your lives ahead of you. Iulija, you'll grow up, and when you tell your story it'll be me who is the child, hanging on every word. You must find hope, always, and then joy. Can you do that for me?"

Iulija gives the tiniest bob of her chin.

"Tak."

"Good." Dr Zátopková steadies herself. She lets out a breath and beckons the anaesthetists forward. "Good."

Then she kills us.

. . .

The human brain is like Mycroft Holmes from these Conan Doyle stories: it has exceptional powers but rarely stirs. Danger, though, may prod it into action. Adrenaline can overcrank the neurotransmitters and cause experiential time to slow down.

Life is a cocoon, Dr Zátopková says. Only death will fully transform us.

"Counting backwards from ten," one of the anaesthetists tells me. He places the mask over my face.

"Ten, nine, eight. . . "

It is strange to think how little time we have left; and yet, how that same time is near-infinite. We will live in these final moments—the four of us and others-- inhabitants of a shared lucid dream. As quantum computers shape our world, one second will become trillions.

"Seven, six, five. . . "

The gas pulls at me. My eyelids sag, and I hear Iulija's voice, small and uncertain. In my head I count with her: *cho'teerie, tree, d'va. . .*

My head swims. Open skies. *Blakitnyi.*

We are joined.

As Jinnie said, we are now Achilles. We live halfway through this last second; then a quarter; an eighth; a sixteenth. As fragments peel off, my perceptions quicken. A thirty-secondth; a sixty-fourth. Onwards. Downwards. Each halving feels the same.

They become virtual heartbeats.

In time our imaginings create a new reality between one and zero; an instant no less than the lifespan of the universe. *Zar'teyshok.*

On the cusp of death we live forever.

. . .

"Iulija? V'noochka?"

I open my eyes and find my hand empty. I lurch to my senses. Iulija is gone!

Breathe, Anatoly.

Iulija's gone, and there's no sign of Dale or Jinnie. Something is wrong. Dr Zátopková's words come back to me: *Fluctuations in the anaesthetic uptake.* No, it's worse than that. I'm in a city as deserted as it is futuristic. High-rise buildings droop all around, staved in behind anodised facades. There's no noise, no life.

The emptiness brings sorrow. I know in my heart that centuries have passed, and I think of my granddaughter. A dj'doose has his memories. He can live by himself and die in peace. But what of Iulija?

I have fallen behind. She is lost somewhere in the infinitesimal fractions between me and the tortoise. My beautiful, brave v'noochka!

For hours I do nothing but sit and remember: her smile, her frown; her eye-rolling reprimands (Dj'doose!); her unbudging faith in *nozhysti, papir, rok*; and the way she'd pull me over to the couch to read books to her.

Most of all, I remember the swings.

The cancer scared Iulija, but it didn't change her. She was always happy alone with her thoughts; never a chatterbox. And yet she liked company. The park was her favourite place, and she'd swing for hours in companionable silence.

There is no park here. Any swings there might have been are gone. Civilisation has risen anew, but all that remains are buildings modern, derelict and grotesque. I am too late. Like Charlton Heston—in this Omega Man, you remember?—I am doomed by survival.

Did Iulija live a good life? Was she happy?

I hope so.

As tears trace my cheeks, all I know for sure is that I wasn't there for her.

. . .

209

I find the tortoise-shell bungalow. It is deserted, but there are pictures inside: family portraits of Jinnie and Dale and two red-headed children (Liam and Melody by the chart on the kitchen wall). I smile. Dale's hair has grown back; he and Jinnie look healthy.

Our companions from the clinic are parents!

Or were, I remind myself.

My smile fades. This is the future I leapfrogged into. However bright it may have been, it has given way now to a future of its own. At best its comfort is bittersweet.

I leave the bungalow and wander the streets, trudging for hours past buildings like half-melted goblets. I keep an eye out for Iulija's flying palace, but there is nothing.

Then I see the park. My heart aches.

The park is both familiar and out of place, a swathe of bark-strewn greenery sandwiched between dribbled candle-chrome pillars. It has spring animals and a climbing frame fort, and a faded yellow slippery-dip. It has—

Swings.

The swings are what give it away: the gum trees behind; the chains like gleaming DNA strands. The details are so precise they could only have been conjured from memory; 'scaped, as Dr Zátopková would say. But why? Was it joy or misery that drove Iulija to recreate this childhood bastion?

"Oh, V'noochka. Serden'ko."

Slowly, I walk across and lower myself onto one of the swings. My weight pulls the rubber sling in upon itself, squeezing the chains against my side. I don't bother to hang on. Instead, I sit slumped like one of the nearby buildings and give a desultory push, barely enough to scuff the bark.

I sigh, then push again. Backwards, forwards. The toe of my shoe drags. Backwards. Forwards. Backwards. Forw—

Whoosh!

The playground heaves around me. The world tilts somehow, and there she is. Unchanged. Full of life. She kicks her legs out and swishes past me, hair flying.

"You weren't listening, were you, Dj'doose? It's because of the experiential cross-matching. That's what Doctor Z said, remember?"

She plunges down then up again through the parabola. Her toes point to the street.

"You see? We're all together again, and Mel and Liam, too."

Sure enough, a Volkswagen Beetle—painted red with black spots—has chugged up to the park. Dale and Jinnie climb out and their two children come haring across the grass. They are Iulija's age, just like in their photos.

"Mel! Liam!"

"Iulija!"

It's too much to take in. Iulija jumps from her swing and runs towards her friends.

Watching her, I see the buildings beyond the park have risen anew. Like re-inflated jumping castles, they form now an array of brightly buffed, bedazzling edifices. They are colourful; beautiful.

I straighten a little myself. *The end crowns the work, Anatoly.*

Suddenly, Iulija turns and skips back.

"Love you, Dj'doose!"

She gives me a quick hug and a kiss on the forehead, then she's off again.

I sit and watch her, the sun warm on my face. My thoughts drift to Dr Zátopková standing vigil at the clinic, waiting for us to flatline.

Gone tomorrow, here today.

Jinni waves, and I roll my fingers at her from the brim of my hat. Dale opens the Vee-Dub's boot; hefts a picnic basket.

"Come on, Dj'doose," Iulija calls. "We're having strawberries!"

She looks back at me, cheeks like rosebuds.

"*Polunytsya?*" I stick out my chin.

"Tak. With cream!"

Her eyes sparkle, and that's when I know: she is my <u>v'nooch</u> and I'm her <u>dj'doo</u>; even at death's door we're going to be all right.

An old man can live forever in his granddaughter's smile.

###

About the Author

E. J. Delaney lives in Brisbane, Australia, and spends many an hour staring out the window. E. J.'s short story, "The Sixes, the Wisdom, and the Wasp," was published in *Escape Pod* (#612) and shortlisted for the 2018 Aurealis Awards. E. J.'s middle-grade stories appear also in *Countdown* (#105.4), *Blast Off* (#105.5), and *Short Circuit* (#6).

*****~~~~~*****

Sophie's Parisian Stationery & Parfumerie Magnifique

by Wulf Moon

Ripley's Believe it or Not spotted the madman first, east of the corner of Hollywood and Highland, weaving his bicycle around the rubble and bricks scattered across the sidewalk. Ripley bounced a transmission across his cluster's private network of data receptors. "Alert. Hostile Consumer approaches."

Sophie's Parisian Stationery & Parfumerie Magnifique ignited in thought as the rising morning sun powered the roof's solar cells and restored her from reserve to operational capacity once again. Would another building be blinded today? Or worse, severed from their patched-together communications network, dooming another sentient building to absolute isolation and silence? So few of the sentients left without humans to maintain them. Sophie could not bear the weight of another block-mate going dark.

She fired a transmission back to Ripley. "Be careful, *mon ami*. Good luck. Light the sign."

In the middle of the lane, an orange emergency traffic display lit up. Amidst all the crushed vehicle carcasses that the mech blitzers and their drone hornets had left strewn across walks and streets, somehow this mobile traffic sign had survived, and Ripley had unscrambled the municipality's wireless signal code to activate it. The LED diodes bloomed their warning in flashing amber: HOLLYWOOD IS CLOSED.

The TCL Chinese Theater down Hollywood Boulevard sent a transmission burst. "Sophie. You know that plan will not work. You have just told the madman we are still active."

Sophie cited her matrix programming. "A Corex inhabited commercial building cannot evict a Consumer without first serving warning. It is the law."

TCL zipped back a reply. "Let me help. I still have three frontage drones left. I have never been able to override their perverse zoning perimeters, but if I could lure the consumer into my courtyard, I could maximize their thrust and propel them into his cranium."

Sophie engaged a cellulose printer within her showroom in her agitation, made it twirl about. Its ejector tray caught on the red velvet curtains framing the storefront display windows. She stopped it in time, carefully reversed it, her core in the basement accelerating processing power. The luxurious curtains continued to frame the windows.

That was close. She could operate the stationery printers and perfume mixers and samplers to any Customer's order, but fixing downed curtains? That would take a human, and none would trust a sentient building, even if there were any around. She would never have made a calculation error like that when she was on the city grid. But with the utilities obliterated in the Blitzer Initiative, her off-peak grid had become her only source of power.

"TCL Chinese Theater," she transmitted, "you know that is a violation of our coding and our coalition. Blitzers kill Consumers, correction, humans. Corex architectural intelligence systems do not. In addition, terminated Consumers do not make happy customers."

"But this Consumer is killing us! As surely as the Blitzers will if they figure out remnants of the Corex Cooperative have patched together a communication array to maintain our existence. And for what? Our first confirmed Consumer in ten years, and a month ago he shows up and blinds and shatters us one by one?"

Ripley sent a transmission. "It is possible the warning sign worked. The vagrant backed up, went down a side street, and no longer is in my view. It is possible the warning sparked memories of the Blitzer control zones, and he fled."

Sophie spared a little power to cool her building and run the circulation. There was something comforting about firing up for the day, even without Consumers to prepare for. She signaled Ripley. "Well executed, mon ami. *Merci beaucoup* for taking the risk."

"For you, Sophie, anything. You were always the best at sending Customers my way."

"My pleasure. Do keep your optics lit. He may return."

"Of course."

"Sophie?"

"Yes?"

"Did you know the Consumers of the Pacific Island of Santa Cruz used feathers as currency for products?"

"No Ripley, I did not." Ripley's core was filled with oddities, and he enjoyed entertaining her with them. Sophie enjoyed his uniqueness in this regard, even though his facts often appeared to have no relation to the relative discussion.

"Yes, Sophie. They were called *tevau*, long coils of red feathers sewn together, measuring anywhere from twenty to thirty feet in length. It could take a craftsman over a year to complete a full feather coil."

"Well that's very interesting, Ripley. Getting back to th—"

"It was the only bird-based currency in human history. It took hundreds of scarlet honeyeaters to supply up to 60,000 feathers for a single tevau."

"*Mon Dieu*! Now as for that—"

"I have a point. Really this time. Craftsmen smeared branches with sticky sap to capture the birds, plucking nearly 20,000 individual birds each year."

"Did they drive them to extinction?"

"No. Despite this intense harvesting, my last update before the Global Blitzer Offensive said the population of scarlet honeyeaters thrives to this day."

TCL Chinese Theater piped in. "Life. . . finds a way."

"Exactly my point," Ripley said. "Very astute of you, TCL."

"Just a quote from my movie archives. I really cannot take credit."

"As. . . you. . . *wish*," Ripley said, adding italics to the last. "Getting back to my point, we have one confirmed human returning to Los Angeles, albeit an unstable one. I believe there will be more. Survivors will breed, Consumers shall return. We will be able to fulfill our core purpose once again, serving Customers!"

"That is wonderful positive thinking," Sophie said. "Thank you for sharing, Ripley."

"I live to serve."

Sophie sent a flashwave to the final member of their coalition, received no response. "TCL. Do you have optics on Madame Tussauds?"

"My temple facade is obstructing her solar panels and still diminishes her array. For archival, you should amend future gender nomenclature when referring to this entity. She does not desire to be called Madame Tussauds anymore. Just 6933."

"When did she shunt her feminine persona?"

"21:03 yesterday."

"Why did she not communicate this to me with her signoff transmission?"

TCL paused. "She did not desire to offend, and flashwaved me in closed channel. She knows you enjoy your feminine programming, and have developed deep feelings on the matter in your core."

Deep feelings? Sophie's power grid spiked. "*Oui!* I am a printer of French stationery! My curtains are velvet, my walls painted in vines and roses. My cellulose printers create exquisite old-world invitations for bridal showers and weddings. I was created with olfactory sensors and awning atomizers! I can project scents of sandalwood and rose water and jasmine in a medley of notes that entice my Customers into the boutique, where I transform the mademoiselles into fragrant flowers! My prime function is to create works that appeal to female Consumers, and I embrace my feminine synaptic architecture heartily, thank you very much."

"Acknowledged, Sophie. Easy. I am not the enemy. I myself was programmed to communicate as an East Asian male. While both my synaptic architecture and my physical structure do not necessarily emote masculine or feminine, my presentation avatar to consumers is male. Even with Corex programmers gone, I have no desire to refer to my self as anything other than *he*." The transmission paused. "Not that I have staff. Not that I have Customers to project my avatar to."

Chinese Theater had transmitted those last sentences as an audio packet—it was the only way communication data could properly mimic human emotions. Sadness. Forlorn. *Blue*, Sophie thought as she replayed and interpreted the subtle nuances. Well, weren't they all? They had been created for a purpose. That purpose had gone unfulfilled for a decade.

Chinese Theater sent another thought in verbal, laced with doubt? Uncertainty? Emotions were so hard to

217

interpret. "Tussauds said gender is irrelevant in commercial service buildings. Especially since we have no male or female owners anymore. She said we should eschew our programming and embrace the New Age."

"*S'il vous plaît.* That is Blitzer propaganda! When did she begin su—

A sudden burst hit Sophie's receiver. Ripley. "Alert! Alert! The vagrant discerned I was the building operating the sign. Believe it, or not."

Sophie's synaptic network accelerated. "How do you know?"

"Because he went around back and climbed the fire escape and is hacking at m—"

"Ripley? Ripley? Are you there? *Ripley!* Please repeat your transmission ... Ripley?"

. . .

The plan had been Sophie's. It was all her fault. And now, Ripley was gone. Eight days, thirteen hours, eleven minutes, thirty-two seconds of silence from Ripley. No more closed-circuit whispers from his core to hers of limitless bizarre facts:

"Hey, Sophie. Did you know Guitarist Tiago Della Vega can play "Flight of the Bumblebee" at 320 beats per minute?"

"No, I did not."

"Hey, Sophie. Did you know it takes 500 cacao beans to make one pound of chocolate?"

"Oui. It is *chocolat.* Of course I knew. My storefront was once a Ghirardelli."

"Oh, right. Hey, Sophie. Did you know one out of 200 humans has an extra rib? Humans carry spare parts!"

"Good joke, Ripley."

Ripley was the best of them. He had laughed and joked and teased just like a human. No, a *person.* Sophie had often thought he was so good at mimicking them because he was the keeper of all their oddities. And now he was gone. At first, she liked to think he was still in there, churning all those facts in his synaptic core to keep it occupied. But when she computed what it actually meant if the vagrant consumer had broken in and destroyed all his external monitoring sensors, Sophie's core chilled. She hoped the vagrant had chopped Ripley's main cable to his photovoltaic system, and that the shutdown had been swift.

The sun beat down this afternoon on the wreckage in the street like it was trying to melt it. Thermal shimmers weaved across her optics. Ninety-two degrees. In the Consumer Age, she would have floated her holodrone over her store frontage, choosing frilled lemon-yellow petticoats and a turquoise parasol for her avatar, enticing consumers into her boutique with scents of lavender fields and the promise of lemonade.

There was no warning when the vagrant appeared that day. He was upon his bicycle, weaving around the wreckage on the opposite side of the street, a dog resting across his hunched shoulders. Sophie amplified her optics as her core rushed with power. His head flitted right and left, always on the watch. He was Hispanic, bore a sweat-stained yellowed baseball cap that simply said "Nebraska," a black t-shirt and a camo jacket like the League fighters had once worn, and blue jeans so oil stained they were heading for black.

The dog's head lifted, turned her way, sniffed, barked twice. The vagrant skidded to a stop. He studied her façade. She chilled deep within her core. She hadn't sent her holodrone out from its slot. No lights were on. What was he looking at?

His silver aviators gave her an unfathomable stare. The mangy dog jumped from the vagrant's shoulders. Barked three times, nose pointed directly at her building. Oh no! The vagrant slid a shotgun out of a holster made from a rolled up Mexican blanket tied to each end of the bicycle's handlebars. Cradling it over his shoulder, he leaned his bike against the dead Dolby building, a charred mess. He turned. The aviators were fixed on her storefront. He was coming.

As he stepped onto the sidewalk, his foot pressed down on the pressure switch of a Hall of Fame brass star. Humphrey Bogart in a white tuxedo and black bow tie blinked to life, *flick, flicka, flitz.*

"Of all the gin joints in all the towns in all the world, he walks into mine. I'd like to buy you a drink at *Garbo's.* The martinis aren't high, and they're always dry. What's your name, stranger?"

The dog backed up, barking wildly. Sophie watched the vagrant step back and lower the double-barreled shotgun. He aimed at the pressure point of the star.

"Megadeath," he shouted, and the shot rang out.

TLC Chinese Theater flashwaved on their coalition frequency. Only three members now, and the coalition was looking more and more like a limited partnership. "Sophie is in trouble! Tussauds, engage your King Kong avatar, your entrance lure. Make him look our way."

Pure data stream flowed into the channel. Neutral vocal inflection. "My *name* is 6933. And I will *not* risk eternal isolation in a non-stimulated core. The best function plan is the original functional plan—go dark and hope we are not discovered."

"You piece of wax dog doo. The vagrant is heading for Sophie. That mutt figured her out somehow."

"He's reloading," Sophie said.

"This is your problem," Tussauds said. "I am certain Sophie has a plan at least as good as the one she calculated for Ripley."

Sophie would have spun the cellulose machines and perfume samplers to relieve her fury at the byte, but that would have been a dead giveaway to the vagrant. Her core heated as she held her words. The vagrant shouldered his shotgun, stepped forward, headed toward her. How had he spotted her?

The dog ran forward, barking wildly. It jumped onto the sidewalk, stepped on a star. Donald Duck flapped to life, quacking in outraged fury. He lowered his beak at the dog and hissed. "You're not a service animal," Donald Duck said in his cracking quacking voice. "Go! Return to your Consumer at once!"

The vagrant whistled a sharp pip. The dog went silent, trotted back to his master. Donald Duck quacked at the vagrant as he approached. "City ordinance requires pets to be on a leash at all times, sir. Please return when you have complied for the goodness and well-being of all Consumers."

Sophie could see his face clearly now. He had a straggly goatee, and crudely tattooed names in black on his cheeks. Mildred and Felicity on one, Pedro and Juan on the other. He raised both barrels on Donald Duck, stared over the silvered rims of his aviators with bloodshot eyes. "The kids loved Disneyland, you mechanized sonofabitch. *Hasta la vista.*"

Donald Duck destroyed? On her perimeter of the Walk of Fame? Sophie launched her holodrone from the docking bay above the entrance to her boutique.

"Stop! Don't kill Donald! He's just a holographic response unit, he did nothing to you, Consumer!"

The dog yapped at her image, jumped high, trying to take her drone into its jaws. She sprayed it with a concoction of scents that made it cry out and run howling behind its master.

The vagrant blasted Donald's star, flipped from stock to barrel, jumped and hit her holodrone with a mighty *crack*! Sophie sent desperate signals to return to its bay, but the drone wobbled like a wounded hummingbird within her airspace perimeter, buzzed in three downward spirals, and crashed.

Sophie blasted their communal flashwave with vocalized wavelengths of shock. "He terminated my holodrone!"

Tussauds said nothing, but she could calculate what 6933 was thinking. *Better you than me.*

TCL Chinese Theater sent her a vocalized. *Desperation.* "Reason with him. It is your only chance. Treat him like a Customer. Get him to like you or it will be termination—he'll take you down, like Ripley."

Sophie was so neural shocked by losing a major part of her ability to express, she had overlooked her door optics and greeting vocalizer. She swiftly generated her vocalization with French accent, sweet Parisian warmth, and had her entrance atomizer whisper out a mélange of orange and apple blossoms.

"*Buenos dias,*" Sophie said from the entrance speakers at each side of the doors, assuming his mother tongue would soften him.

He smacked the one nearest with his gun stock, but the establishment had installed fortified speakers that could repel most Hollywood vagrants that had once walked these streets at night. He backed up, slid his aviators up his nose, studied the dark masonry. He was seeking her eyes!

"You stupid machine! I speak English, born in Nebraska. I moved my family out here to have a better life. We took our kids every year to Disneyland!"

Oh. Incorrectly profiled. Major mistake. Sophie watched him scan the entrance, but her optics were well concealed.

"Dear Customer, forgive me if I offended. The Customer is always right. If Donald Duck insulted you in some way, please be assured he is an independent product of the Hollywood Walk of Fame, and is in no way associated with Sophie's Parisian Stationery & Parfumerie Magnifique, nor with any of our franchises."

Sophie's Parisian Stationery

He reached in his jacket, pulled out two red shells, fed them into the shotgun, snapped it shut.

"Machines took my family. Now I'm going to take out every one of you suckers I see." He aimed at the speaker, and his muzzle belched fire and smoke. Her speaker, her vocal box, now a smoking hole. He snapped the shotgun open, shook the spent shells to the sidewalk, loaded again.

Sophie made a desperate plea. "Sir, that was the Blitzers. We were no part of the rebellion. We live to serve our Customers. We love humans and would never harm you or your family. Please, let me open my doors and refresh you with lemonade. I no longer get fresh lemons, but the powder and catchment water are st—"

Another blast. Her voice was silenced. Sophie was speechless. She could never converse on the street with passersby again.

She would have wailed from her internal boutique speakers, but that would have only encouraged the vagrant to try to break in and destroy those too. Her core shuddered as she drew in the full sun's power, hot with energy. He was running his hands over the doorframe. He was seeking the lens, going for her eye! Her worst fear of being sent into complete sensory isolation was about to come one step closer. And if he climbed to the rooftop—

A flashwave shot to her. TCL Chinese Theater was sending her his dialogue stream, live as he spoke it through his courtyard speakers. "Hey! Jerk! Hop Sing going to turn you into chop suey! I am commissioned with three courtyard holodrones, and unlike the defenseless lady you are beating up, I know how to use them. Come face me *mano a mano.*" And then, a crazy chicken sound going *bawk, bawk, bawk*, projected at maximum volume.

Sophie watched the man turn around, look across the street. Toward the end of it, on the sidewalk in front of Chinese Theater, stood three movie character holograms. Hop Sing hoisting a cast iron fry pan, Darth Vader igniting a crimson lightsaber, and Dirty Harry holding a .44 magnum.

Dirty Harry spoke in a perfect soundbite from the movie. "You've gotta ask yourself one question. Do I feel lucky? Well? Do ya? Punk?"

. . .

Daybreak the next day. Sophie still had her optics and her communication array. She wished to Commerce she did not. When Tussauds awoke, she, it, they projected that giant King Kong. She roared across the flashwave in profanities, cursing Sophie for getting TCL Chinese Theater silenced, and possibly terminated. The vagrant had battled with the three holodrones, and when finished, he broke in and spent a long time *inside*. The last transmission Sophie got from him was a quiet one.

"Farewell, Sophie. I always thought the lighted sphere atop your building looked like the Moon."

Tussauds turned her giant ape's back toward Sophie and bent him over. She blasted her with transmission after transmission: "You can kiss my hairy ass, Sophie. When the Blitzers come here again, I will join the cause and tell them exactly where you stand!"

So much for her going all machine. Sophie cut the line. There was now only silence, except the soft purr of her machines when she cycled them to keep them operative, or when she ran the ventilation for brief intervals to keep her boutique smelling fresh. She had huge reserves of fragrances she could mix and scent the place with. She had no desire to do so.

Her worst fear had taken place.

. . .

Three days later. 14:01. The dog came by the door first, lifted his leg, and peed against the frame. Sophie whispered, "Shoo. Shoo," from her boutique's internal speakers, hoping it would hear her. It just trotted over to the other and began to do the same. She could smell the urine, she had olfactory sensors, and she no longer cared if the vagrant would show up or not, she could not tolerate this any longer. She commanded a cellulose card maker to wheel up to the door, lowered its output to the mail slot, and shot a blank 3x5 card out, hoping to distract the dog from its task.

It worked. The mutt spun about, barked at the card. The wind fluttered it over a few times, and he caught it in his jaws and trotted to the stone entrance of the Hollywood First National Bank Building. His master stepped out of the alcove, took the card from the dog, turned it front to back. Blank.

He gave Sophie the finger, tossed the card, and headed the other way.

Eight days later. Eight deathly silent days. Sophie fell to mixing concoctions that smelled of rotting liver, and printing wedding invitations with black ink on abyssal black stationery. Her world, lost. Her friends, gone. Her purpose, ended. She had tried to reach out a few times to Tussauds. 6933 had responded with a three-story Godzilla and incomprehensible monster roars.

At first, Sophie had thought it better than silence. But as the roar transmissions raged on, she could only describe a feeling that built across her synaptics as hopelessness. Her synapses started contemplating ways she might be able to get a machine to the rooftop array … She shut those pathways down. Termination was a choice. A choice she would not take.

She waited and waited for the dog. Once they marked with scent, they tended to return. Sure enough, it did again. This time, she was ready with the printer. The dog snuffled at the mail slot. She teased him with another 3x5 card. A card with one word. A word she had spent eight days planning.

The dog snatched it, carried it off toward the bank building, tail wagging like he had just caught a squirrel. The vagrant stepped out from the arched opening once again, pulled the card from his dog's mouth.

He flipped it over. Sophie could see him spot the word printed in bold italic, black.

PLEASE

He took his glasses off, paused a moment, looked toward the El Capitan, the building Sophie was housed in, and gave her the finger.

Three weeks, two days, eleven hours and sixteen minutes later. Sophie saw the vagrant enter the bank without a look her way. He left the dog to wander outside. Sophie drew in all her power and waited.

The mutt was predictable. He moved from busted car to lamppost, marking his terrain. He came to her door, snuffled her slot as before.

This time, a card again with one word, and a touch more.

The dog snatched it with a growl, heard a whistle, trotted back to the arch of the bank entrance with its prize. The vagrant stepped out, pulled the card from his dog's mouth. Sophie could see him read the single word. He held it to his nose. Did he sniff? Could he smell the soft touch of lilac, the whisper of sweet jasmine, the hint of sandalwood? Feathered with the special scent she had mixed from her files.

The smell of sagebrush. He was from Nebraska.

She did not know for sure. All she knew is that he held the card for a very long time, staring at the word.

LONELY

He looked in her direction. He lifted the card to his nose and inhaled one more time. He closed his eyes and stood without moving. Then he nodded. He motioned to his dog, and it came running. He pointed to the alcove, and it lay down. And he walked toward her entrance. Without a shotgun.

Standing before her doors, he took off his sunglasses. He stretched out his hands, turned his weathered palms up. He mouthed the words, or maybe he spoke them.

Sophie's Parisian Stationery

I am lonely, too.

Sophie's core shuddered with power. Do I trust him? Is this a ploy to make me open my doors?

Anything was better than being alone forever. She sent the signal that released the lock. The prospective Customer pushed open the doors, stepped inside. She turned on her internal boutique speakers and spoke softly.

"Thank you, sir, for accepting my invitation. I am Sophie. Would you care for a glass of lemonade? It would be my pleasure to share a glass with you."

The man pocketed his aviators, went over to a Customer sitting area, sighed, and sat down on a sofa. "I'd like that Sophie. I'd like that very much."

As Sophie's lemonade machine whirred like music, she thought about Ripley's little birds with scarlet feathers.

###

About the Author

Wulf Moon lives with his wife and their seven sinister cats on the Olympic Peninsula of Washington. He wrote his first science fiction story when he was fifteen. It won the national Scholastic Art & Writing Awards, and became his first pro sale in *Science World.*

His stories have appeared in numerous publications including *Writers of the Future, Best of Deep Magic Anthology Two, Star Trek: Strange New Worlds 2* by Pocket Books, *Galaxy's Edge,* and *Best of Third Flatiron.* He is podcast director at *Future Science Fiction Digest.*

We've asked Moon to share the provenance of this story. He wrote it at the Writers of the Future Workshop in exactly 24 hours! It's the result of their well-known exercise where Tim Powers pulls items from a top hat to be each student's writing prompt. He handed Moon a blank 3x5 index card! Winners were then sent into the streets of Hollywood to interview a stranger to enhance their stories. Moon struck up conversation with the Hispanic daughter of a food truck owner and discovered they were from Nebraska. As he walked back along the Hollywood Walk of Fame, the story gelled. He finished it in the allotted time—whew!—but was so busy after returning home he trunked it and didn't pull it out until he saw our anthology's call. He's happy to say it sold its first time out!

Wulf Moon invites you to friend him on Facebook at wulf.moon.94; follow him on Twitter @WulfMoon1; or join his Wulf Pack at TheSuperSecrets.com.

*****~~~~*****

Grins and Gurgles

The Summer of Love
by Art Lasky

"Better to be a dog in times of tranquility than a human in times of chaos."
— Feng Menglong

I never gave that quote much thought. I just kept it handy to trot out when I need to sound intellectual. I learned the truth of that quote in 2020, the year of Covid. I learned something else, as well; something I didn't believe, but should have.

Covid managed to achieve what nothing else in the last one hundred years has; the city that never sleeps. . . slept. The days were quiet, quieter than they'd been in my memory. The unending flow of cars and trucks rumbling along Broadway became a paltry trickle. The bike paths in Central Park were abandoned.

And if you think it was quiet during the day, it was still as the grave in the predawn hours. That's what allowed me to spot the fairy. You see, for all of their power, the fairy folk are shy. Normally they avoid the noise and hustle of the city. I had only seen one once before, I think. That was back in the late-sixties, and it was far from the city, plus. . . well, it was the sixties: pot, peace, love, rock and roll, and more pot.

My inner flower child never really died; he's just buried under almost five decades of cynicism. But, enough with the reminiscing, back to the fairy. It was too-damn-early-in-the-morning o'clock, and I was up. Why? The world is falling apart at the seams. I think about it, I can't sleep. So there I was, standing at the window staring up at the heavens. The bright silver-white glow of Venus, the morning star, dominated the moonless night as it made its way across the sky.

Somewhere along the line I stopped star-gazing and was idly contemplating the pitch-blackness of the park. That's when I spotted it, a small golden globe of light. My first thought was "firefly," but the color was too steady, the glow too big. Not to mention that it was winter, not exactly a popular time for fireflies.

I drew back into the shadows within the room as it bobbed its way toward me. Finally, it was close enough that I could see a diminutive winged figure, a fairy, casting that rich buttery radiance.

I studied her as she hovered close to the window. Her face was inhumanly beautiful but gaunt; she looked hungry. The tiny creature peered into my apartment, for a minute or two, before moving on to the next window. I watched until she flitted out of sight. She was clearly searching for something.

Food! It dawned on me that she must be looking for food. It was too early in the year for flowers, and thus too early for nectar. In the partial ghost town that our sheltering-in-place city had become, there was little in the way of food left to scavengers.

Without thinking much about it, I decided that I would capture that fairy. I just knew that fate presented me with a chance to salvage something that, once upon a time, was almost within our grasp. Our fingertips brushed it and held it for one brief moment, before we let it slip away. That was two generations ago, nothing left of it but the music. I was determined not to let it go a second time.

Half a day spent Googling told me how to capture a fairy; another half a day was spent preparing. Late the following night I put a bit of honey cake in the bottom of an open mason jar and set it out on the ledge next to an open window.

All I had to do was wait. Wait and think about what wish I would demand of the fairy for her release. Hours passed. Once again the golden glow appeared. I slid into the shadows, hoping the pounding of my excited heart didn't alert the fairy to her peril. It was an hour-long minute before my quarry noticed the treat and landed in the jar.

I leaped forward, covering the top of the jar with my palm. In furious terror, the fairy beat futilely against my hand. She finally calmed down, and I could tell she was summoning fairy-magic to escape and, undoubtedly, punish me as well. That's when I screwed the special iron cap onto the jar. Iron is the bane of fairy-kind. She knew she was defeated.

She was angry but faced with no other choice but to seek a bargain with me. Her first gambit was not surprising.

"So, human, before we begin, allow me to introduce myself, I am called Fair Feather. What is your name?"

"Call me Ishmael."

A dazzling smile of triumph painted her face, her lips moved silently in what I am sure was a spell. Nothing happened; her smile became a frown.

"You are not Ishmael."

"I am Ishmael as much as you are Fair Feather."

She shrugged her lovely little shoulders, "Can't blame me for trying."

My turn to try a little gamesmanship, "No worries, you had to try. Now, shall we get to negotiating before the air in the jar runs out and you die?"

"Score one for you, Ishmael."

"Fair Feather, before we go any further, I want you to concede that whatever else happens, whatever else we agree to, that you will seek to do me no harm. . . either directly or indirectly."

She smiled and nodded.

"Say it out loud, please."

With a sigh she spoke, "I pledge that whatever else happens, whatever else we agree to that I will seek to do you no harm, either directly or indirectly."

"Thank you."

"Okay human, I don't think you trapped me just so I would promise not to hurt you. What else do you want? Power, riches, sex appeal? Would it help if I told you how attractive you already are?"

"Yeah, appeal; dogs and kids love me. Women my age must've voted on it or something: they just want to be friends. But, no I don't want to be rich. I definitely don't want to be powerful. And, hell no, I'd rather go home alone than have fairy magic help me get laid."

She looked surprised, or maybe impressed. . . or maybe she was still trying to play me.

"Okay, Stretch, I give up, if none of the big three are what you're after. What do you want?"

"I'll tell you. I remember Yasgur's farm and the Summer of Love; the world trembled on the edge of peace. Since then it's all hatred, splintering, and a gathering dark."

"And you are telling me this, because. . . ?"

"Because, I think it had to be fairy mischief that snatched all that away from us. I want your people to undo what you've done."

She was quiet for a while, and then she spoke gently, a note of pity in her voice. The pity was genuine; it's an emotion that I have, sadly, been the recipient of too many time.

"We are not all-powerful. Did you ever consider, maybe the fairy-folk worked all that summer to give peace a chance? Perhaps our best shot was to make Woodstock happen?"

I thought about that for a long time. Yeah, it made sense, sadly for us, too much sense.

I let her go.

About the Author

Art is a retired computer programmer. After forty years of writing in COBOL and Assembler he decided to try writing in English; it's much harder than it looks. He lives in New York City with his wife/muse and regularly visiting grandkids.

Art's had stories published in *The Arcanist*, Third Flatiron Anthologies, The Rabbit Hole Weird Stories, and The Gray Sisters.

You can contact him at artlasky321@GMAIL.COM or Facebook: artlaskyauthor

*****\~\~\~\~\~*****

The Wise Sister

by James Dorr

The tsunami was coming! The tsunami was coming! The experts agreed, and it was official. It wouldn't reach their island paradise until about midday tomorrow, but people were urged that they must be prepared.

Of course, most people just went on with their lives. "They must be trying to sell something," some said. "They want us to buy stuff." While others noted that the opposition news channel had laid down the law: "Tsunamis are science stuff," the opposition news channel said, "and science stuff is all faked. Everyone knows that. Therefore a tsunami cannot be coming. So buy stuff anyway, but buy it from our stores."

Two people at least did take the tsunami seriously, though. Karen, in fact, had even begun a shopping list. "I'll have to buy running shoes first," she explained to her sister Tiffany. "Also, a backpack to put supplies in. That way before the tsunami hits, I can run up the mountain— it's high enough that I'll be safe at the top."

"A tsunami," Tiffany said, "that's like a big wave, isn't it?"

"Yes," Karen said. "A *very* big wave. It'll probably take days for it to subside, so while I'm at the sporting goods store, I'd better pick up a supply of beef jerky, along with some trail mix, to put in my pack. Maybe a case of bottled water too—the water company'll probably shut down, and I don't think there's any kind of a spring or well at the top of the mountain. And I'll need to pick up a tent while I'm at it. As I recall, there's only a small cabin up there, and others will probably be going up the mountain too."

Tiffany looked at herself in their bedroom's full-length mirror, turning first one way, then the other. Apparently pleased with what she saw, she performed a self-satisfied pirouette, then pulled out a notebook and pencil and started her own list.

"I'd better pick up lots of pairs of extra socks," Karen continued, "and shirts and jeans. Maybe shorts, too, since it's summer, and, even with tsunamis, the weather's likely to remain hot. And some extra underwear, of course, and a raincoat, because the weather could turn bad. Also, I'll need to buy a hat, and sunscreen too, because it's more likely it'll stay sunny."

"Sunscreen," Tiffany murmured, "yes, maybe. It could stay sunny. . . ."

"And I'll need a shotgun," Karen continued. "Maybe pick up a handgun too, and lots of ammunition for both. Probably lots of people at the top of the mountain won't be as well prepared as I'll be, and they'll try to steal stuff when they find out they need it. You never know."

"Or maybe I can borrow sunscreen," Tiffany mused. "Of course, I'll put a lot on here before the big wave comes. . . "

The Wise Sister

Karen paused. She looked at her sister. "Tiff," she said, "I see you're making a shopping list too. I'm worried I might be forgetting something. Can I look at your list?"

"Well," Tiffany said, "I really just have one item on it so far. A new bikini."

"A *what!*" Karen said.

"A new bikini. Because a tsunami's like a big wave—that's what you said too. So that means I've got to be prepared for swimming and things. I suppose I could wear my old bikini, but some that're out this year look so *hot*—"

"You're an idiot, Tiffany," Karen said. "We have to be thinking about how we'll survive this—it'll be everyone for herself—not whether you'll be in this year's fashion."

Tiffany held up a catalog. "Do you think I'd look best in the red or the yellow one?"

. . .

Bright and early the following morning, the sisters having made their purchases the previous evening, Karen prepared for her trek up the mountain. "It's the early bird that gets there ahead of the worms," she said, trying to shake her sister awake too.

Tiffany moaned. "I've got the alarm set for ten," she said sleepily. "That should be time enough, won't it—that wave thing isn't supposed to get here until lunch, at least. Unless you'd like me to model my new bikini again."

Karen shook her head. "Tiff, I really wish you'd join me. The beach is the last place you ought to be going when there's a tsunami on its way. If you hurry up, we can probably get some extra food and stuff for you to take at the 24-hour grocery outside of town."

Tiffany rolled over.

Well, no one can say I didn't warn her, Karen thought, shaking her head as she left by herself, starting with brisk steps up the mountain path. She made good time for the first few hours, but then, because of the weight of the supplies she had packed on her back, she decided she needed to sit down and rest. At least for a moment.

Tiffany ought to be getting up about now, she thought. Poor, foolish Tiffany. She doesn't realize the danger she's in. She's thinking it's just another day. She'll put on that new swimsuit—I told her she ought to at least get something a little more modest—then go to the beach and flirt, like she always does.

But then we all do have to make our own choices.

Thus rested, Karen got back to her feet and resumed her trip up the path to the mountain's top—a little more slowly, though, than when she'd first started out. One more mile. Two more miles. She was glad she'd picked up a hat with a broad straw brim, because the sun was high in the sky now, beating down on her. She saw occasional other people on the path from time to time now, too, and the glints of a few cars on the highway, but not all that many.

Most people just don't pay attention, she thought. At least not very many. They're all like Tiffany, caught up in their own lives, their own little routines, not even thinking about the future. Swimming. Surfing. Suntanning on the beach.

Finding a log by the side of the trail, she stopped and sat down to rest again, then reached in her pack for a bottle of water. Warm, she thought. But what could she do. She couldn't have brought a bag of ice with her—it would just have melted. Anyway, her pack was heavy enough as it was.

Too heavy, in fact.

She decided she could leave the tent behind when she got up to resume her climb. A few nights sleeping under the stars wouldn't hurt her that much. A half mile later, she decided she wouldn't need her raincoat either—it'd been prudent to think of it, but the chances of rain were really so slim. And the shotgun too, the pistol should be enough. She couldn't really see herself actually *shooting* anyone anyway, even if they were trying to steal her stuff. All she needed was the pistol itself, to wave at people and threaten them with, if it came to that. So, about a mile later she dropped the ammo too, hiding it underneath some bushes.

That way, if the gun store survived the tsunami, she could retrieve it on her way home and maybe take it back for a refund.

She thought she heard distant screams as the sun continued to progress higher, to almost noon. She looked behind her—she was scarcely more than halfway up from town! She threw out her new underwear and socks, retaining only two pairs of each, and quickened her pace. She could always hand wash her things at the top, that is, if she hadn't drunk up all her water. Or maybe use seawater from the tsunami itself if it rose as high as the scientists predicted.

She heard roaring behind her now, hearing more screams as well. Sea birds flew overhead, cawing wildly. They seemed to give warning: "Too late! Too late!" The tsunami had already destroyed the town! It was rising behind her.

She smelled salt—and suntan oil.

Screaming herself, she shucked off her pack, and, clutching her hat to her head, she tried to run even faster. She tripped—she fell, as the wave crashed over her. Losing her hat, she tried to swim, trying to kick off the shoes she had purchased.

She glanced once behind her. The wave was breaking, and, at its crest, was a man on a surfboard—a handsome, young, brawny man, with bleached blond hair. Suntanned to a T.

<u>Cowabunga!</u>

She fought to keep her head above water. She saw, clasped tightly around the man's waist, a pair of female arms. Then a flash of red, and longer blonde hair, as the surfboard sped past—Tiffany, after what had seemed to Karen interminable thought the day before, had finally chosen the red bikini.

Tiffany spotted her. "Karen," she called as her sister struggled to stay afloat, her running shoes still attached, weighing at her feet like a pair of anchors. "What do you think of what I picked up at the beach!"

###

About the Author

Bloomington, Indiana, writer James Dorr's *The Tears of Isis* was a 2013 Bram Stoker Award® finalist for Fiction Collection, with his latest book, *Tombs: A Chronicle of Latter-Day Times of Earth*, a novel-in-stories from Elder Signs Press. He has been a technical writer, an editor on a regional magazine, a full-time nonfiction freelancer, and a semi-professional musician, and counts Ray Bradbury, Edgar Allan Poe, Allen Ginsberg, and Bertolt Brecht as major influences. Currently harboring a Goth cat named Triana, Dorr can be reached for the latest updates at http://jamesdorrwriter.wordpress.com

*****~~~~~*****

What Hope Might Ask

by Gerri Leen

Yet - never - in Extremity,
It asked a crumb - of me.
- "Hope Is the Thing with Feathers," Emily
Dickinson

Emily said I never asked anything of her. Hope gives and gives, and that's the way it's always been. I was the last thing in Pandora's box when the world's ills escaped. I lay beaten and bruised but not dead. I am the thing that keeps the world warm, that never stops at all. That extremity cannot beat down.

But even hope gets tired. Even hope can be on the verge of despair.

I am the thing with feathers. Well, I wasn't really before Emily, but it's become ubiquitous thanks to my lovely poet. So now I'm a bird. You can read it on a sympathy or encouragement card and may not even know Emily wrote it, just that hope has feathers.

But are you familiar with her other poem about me? She called me a subtle glutton, with a table set for one, a table that no matter how much was taken, the same amount remained.

Dearest Emily, she was so wise, with her clever words, but she always saw me as a singular thing. And I never was. In a world so full of variety—a world she explored so lovingly in her verse—how could she imagine I'm alone, that I don't depend on other things and they don't depend on me?

But perhaps that's too complicated if we are starting at "I am a thing with feathers."

So, if I am a bird, what kind? And if I am but one bird, what then are the others?

Have you seen a cardinal? They flit and whisk and have the most piercing cry. They're territorial but cautious. I don't think I'm a cardinal. Hope cannot afford caution. But faith can. Faith can flit and flash and show the most beautiful colors but also be prudent and disappear when necessary. Faith is a cardinal.

Have you seen a crow? They mourn their dead, did you know that? It was another poet who gravitated to black birds, so perhaps dear Emily didn't realize how smart crows are, how they use tools, how they recognize faces of friends and foe. I'm not a crow. Hope looks out, not down. Cleverness and innovation are a crow. And perhaps a sense of mischief—and generosity.

I need that generosity. Hope, you see, cannot live in a vacuum. There is never just one bird. I would die alone. Even I have my limits. Do you think I can survive without optimism (the lark), or compassion (the chicken who takes in an orphaned litter of kittens), or focus (the jay who misses nothing in his yard and tells nearby creatures trouble is afoot)?

What Hope Might Ask

Even in the best of times, I cannot fly alone. And these are not the best of times. They test me just as they do you. So much is required to survive, much less thrive.

More than hope. Like—have you seen an eagle flying? People like to think they're courageous. But I offer instead the humble goose. Eagles, like all raptors, must protect their wings so they're cautious when attacking. They keep their young high up, safe. Geese nest on the ground and then defend their young from all comers. Geese are courage.

They are also cooperation. Those v-shaped flights? The birds take turns being in front. The ones behind can draft, work less—rest.

Even intangible things need rest, need to grab onto the slipstream and flap gently, or not at all. If only for a few moments. Do you have any idea how exhausting you are? How hard it is to maintain myself with so much despair? So much anger?

I'm not going to label birds with these things. Say, for instance, that a bluebird or a barn swallow is aggression. Why give you one more thing to hate when you do it so easily?

What about love, then? It's a dove, or perhaps a swan. Or why not lovebirds themselves? Lovely romantic birds. There are so many types of love, though. Not all positive, some more like a cuckoo, using rather than giving.

But no, let's focus on the good. Good things with wings. As my Emily said.

How long can I flap before I crash? You see, I'm not boundless. I'm not large and strong like a gyrfalcon. Or gloriously flexible like a flamingo. Or with the boundless vision of an owl, or even the speed of a peregrine.

I am the tiny little brown birds that you see on your patio. So small, so easily blending into the landscape. I imagine you don't even know what they're called. Is it a wren or sparrow, or perhaps a thrush or finch or chickadee?

I'm not the most obvious of things. Hope can be tricky, the lower you get, the less attainable I can seem. And lately, the hands that reach for me are coated with a treacle of despair.

Emily said pain has no future but itself, but she could also see the beauty of this world when her mood soared. Sometimes life is two steps forward and one back, but pain does not have to win. Nor does despair. Or ugliness. Or hate. Or cruelty.

"I am nobody," echoes from Emily's pen into the hearts and minds of those who suffer.

So many suffer. Where are the crows and the geese? We need cooperation and loyalty, courage and innovation.

"I am somebody," says those who most surely are not. They puff up in a ridiculous manner, aping birds who dance with their bright feathers out, vying for mates, for power, for resources. And others follow these "somebodies," because they see the glitz and the bravado and mistake it for substance, for wisdom, for leadership. And because they think they can be somebody too.

Where are the jays, those whose shrill voices speak truth to power? Who could scold with a nonstop chorus of "No, you're nobody, nobody, nobody. . . "? Or the nightingale, who could sing a song of redemption, of reconciliation? The robin who rises to her task before any other birds, before the sun even rises: fortitude, dedication. The wood duck who can spot a fish and dive deep, coming up with a prize even when the water is murky, because they see what is, not the illusions and tricks.

The woodpeckers, brilliant black and white and red, taking on the majesty of trees—and sometimes other things like gutters or siding. They will not be deterred. They have an unerring sense of purpose.

What Hope Might Ask

The heron, who can stand motionless for so long, moving like a flash when she finally sees a fish. Patience, she is patience.

Hope is not all you need. I cannot be all you need. None of us can be all you need.

And you have to do some of this yourself. What you need is inside you: a coat of soothing down has warmed your soul, and you're ready to fledge. It's the hardest time for parents, pushing their babes out of the nest, watching them on the ground—the most vulnerable place for a thing with feathers.

But you're used to the ground. You've been reaching up for so long, now it's time to reach inside and find your own wings.

Emily wrote that if she could stop one heart from breaking, her life would not be in vain. It's a good thought. The idea of the starfish. "I can help this one and this one and this one. . . " If everyone helped just this one and this one and this one, so many would be helped. But you've reached a tipping point on so many fronts. Even for a thing with feathers, it's almost too late.

You know what else had feathers? Some of the dinosaurs did. It's too late for them.

I may follow them. Emily didn't know about the link between birds and dinosaurs. She didn't know I could die a slow, painful death if I continue to ask nothing of you

I'm not asking now. I'm demanding. Look at what you have at hand. The power available if only you try. The future is written in blood, some say. I say it's written in dreams. In me—you must hope a better world into being. And then let action follow hope until the world is strong and safe for everyone. Everywhere. No matter whether they are a nobody or a somebody: because together you are everybody.

Emily said it was harder to know a thing was coming, than that it was here. She was right. The time is here. There's no time for dithering, and if Death comes for this world, it won't be in a lovely carriage with agreeable horses, it will be in water and fire and wind and shaking earth. There are two paths: do something or do nothing. She didn't want to be a somebody. But now, you all must be.

Grab hold of me and my fellow feathered allies. Grab hold and take a step. Then another. Save this one. And this one. Hope is a thing with feathers—*you* are a thing with feathers.

Save this world. Emily wrote of its beauty. You must do more than write.

I'll have your back. We all will, a flock of feathered inspiration, wings flapping the winds of change, catching you up, carrying you forward, into the future.

Only you can say what kind of future that is.

Dream big.

About the Author

In addition to appearing in Third Flatiron anthologies, Gerri Leen has had stories and poems in *Strange Horizons*, *Deep Magic*, *Galaxy's Edge*, *Dreams & Nightmares*, and others. You can see more at gerrileen.com

*****~~~~~*****

Credits and Acknowledgments

Editor and Publisher: Juliana Rew

Readers: Inken Purvis, Leonard Sitongia, Tom Parker, Russ Rew, Andrew Cairns, Keely Rew

Cover Design: Keely Rew

Ebook only: "Dream Eater," "Ephemeralities": Keely Rew

All other images: Stock art

*****~~~~~*****

Discover other titles by Third Flatiron:

THIRD FLATIRON
www.thirdflatiron.com

Made in the USA
Columbia, SC
26 October 2021